THE BOUNDARY OF BLOOD

A Novel

CLIFF GRAHAM

Kavod Press

DEDICATION

For every man who has ever been broken.

PREFACE

"In the days of Shamgar son of Anath . . .
the highways were abandoned;
travelers took to winding paths.
Villagers in Israel would not fight . . ."

JUDGES 5:6-7

PROLOGUE

IN HONOR *of the tenth year of the reign of Solomon, son of David, king in Jerusalem, servant of the Most High God Yahweh.*

Hear, oh Israel, Yahweh is God. Yahweh is One.

I, Jehoshaphat, historian of the court, have been commissioned to record chronicles of the warriors of Israel for you, great king.

They were the men of renown who fought to give our people this land. They journeyed through deserts with Moses, conquered with Joshua, judged the tribes, and obeyed Yahweh our God.

Your father shed the blood necessary to establish your throne, and, praise be to God, you will never need to join soldiers on campaign in foreign lands. We are grateful for the prosperity you have cultivated, but I must confess that it brings me regrets.

Troubling whispers haunt the palace corridors. You have stopped seeing your counselors. You no longer meet frequently with your generals. You spend most of your days in the harem.

At the risk of incurring your wrath, great king, you must learn to listen to important truths, even if you do not want to hear them. Your father had many failures, but he always listened to his counselors, and he always sought the favor of our Mighty God. I advise you to do the same.

Your father's hands were calloused by war. Yours are soft with oil and perfume. Though wise beyond compare, you are not possessed with infi-

nite knowledge, and your unwillingness to follow your father's example will make you weak.

You will never know what it is like sitting near a campfire the night before a desperate battle. The camaraderie. The tales being spun of laughter and bravery, and of quiet fear. Yahweh is closest in those moments.

This is my effort to tell you their stories, and perhaps in the telling of them, it will be as though you are there next to the flames, smelling the good smell of wood smoke, listening to the roaring laughs and wondering whether you will earn your seat at tomorrow night's fire.

~

I HAVE CHOSEN to tell you the story of Shamgar son of Anath.

He was one of those who judged the people in the days after Joshua. I believe there is much for you to learn from him.

During this age of prosperity in our kingdom, established by the sword of your father, it is easy to forget what our ancestors suffered; therefore it is important to give you a description of the enemy at the time of the following events.

Your mighty father brought the cities of Philistia to their knees, and now their kings present themselves to you as vassals, their faces pressed against the floor of your golden throne room with your foot on their necks.

But it was not always this way.

Centuries ago, the Five Cities on the coast had all power in the region. Philistine kings ruled our lands from these cities, and the tribes of our father Jacob suffered many lifetimes under the Philistine yoke.

The Philistines were not conquerors like Egypt, bringing with them the order and protection they enjoyed in their own lands. They stole our crops every spring and our people starved, but they did not stay, and whenever they left our hills after plundering and raping, vicious bandits emerged. No one could travel freely on the roads.

As this tale begins, the Israelites are leaderless. They have not been *allowed to possess weapons by their Philistine overlords, and men of Israel must beg for tool repairs from Philistine smiths.*

These events occur at a narrow pass in the mountains near the city of Azekah, at the top of the Elah valley. Your father knew it well and killed the Philistine giant Goliath there.

It is a place where many of our sons have been cut down, because it is the last place invaders can be stopped.

It is a place where the women of Israel shiver with fear at the mention of its name.

Here, mothers become childless.

Here, wives become widows.

It is called the Boundary of Blood.

PART I

❧   I   ❧

IN OUR LAND, storms come from the west.

They build over the Great Sea, cross the cedar-dense forests of Lebanon, and roll through the plains of Philistia, gaining power as they climb into the hill country.

Rain can last for days. Every stream becomes a torrent. Every slope a cascade of rushing water, destroying crops and washing out roads.

In winter, snow gathers quickly and heavily in the mountains. Animals freeze to death, as do unfortunate travelers caught unaware. Those who dwell here can only hide and wait for it to end.

On this night, the storm sends wind ahead of it.

Flowing through the canyons of the Elah valley, tossing tree boughs and stirring up snow already on the ground, it climbs, roils, and rages up from the plains as though sent by an unseen hand from the sea. It finally reaches a small house in the woods at the edge of a field, and as it blows against the house, it rattles the window shutters, waking up a farmer named Shamgar.

He is grateful for this because it has saved him from a terrible dream. His body is drenched in sweat. His breathing comes in short gasps. A strange, paralyzing fear grips him.

He has been having these nightmares every night for a month but seems to forget the details when morning comes. All he remembers is terror and helplessness, and a man who hunts him for no reason.

The shutters continue clattering. He feels his wife stirring next to him, and this encourages him to get up.

He walks quietly to the front door. Putting on his cloak and slipping on his boots, he opens the latch as gently as he can and steps outside.

The trees are shaking violently. The snow that fell the previous day is blowing so hard along the ground that it pelts his face with bits of ice.

It takes him a moment to realize why everything seems . . . odd.

He looks up at the sky.

It is clear. No clouds overhead. But the moon has turned the color of blood, casting a red glow on the snow and red shadows in the forest. The land is bathed in the eerie light. He wonders if he is still in the nightmare.

After watching the moon a moment, he walks around the corner of the house and finds the loose shutter. He picks up a stone and braces the shutter closed, then hurries back inside.

He latches the door shut behind him and stands in the quiet darkness.

A blood moon. A god is angry.

Something inside his mind urges him to put his hand on the latch, open it, and go outside again.

He studies his field. Large enough to hold goats for a week in summer while they are milked for cheese, and large enough for his oxen team to graze in spring after plowing in the valley. Quail nest here all summer, and his traps reliably catch them. Ten years ago he built the fence around the field and removed every stump in it, then built the house himself in time for his wedding. He knows every rock and tree.

CHAPTER 1

He looks around. Besides the weather and the red glow, all appears normal.

But it feels like something is wrong, so he waits.

The last time there was a blood moon, his living children had not yet been born. He wonders if he should wake them up to see it, then decides against it. Long day tomorrow. He will need to plead for the children, plead for everything else precious to him. Perhaps that is what caused the nightmare tonight.

He rubs his eyes and searches around the meadow one more time, unable to shake the feeling of being watched. He looks left and right. The forest is dense. Even in winter, with the undergrowth barren of leaves, it forms a black wall at the edge of the meadow.

Nothing.

A strong gust shakes him as he returns to the front door. He reaches out and touches the door latch.

He hesitates, then turns around and looks at the meadow.

A man is standing at the edge of the forest.

Shamgar calmly turns, lifts the door latch, and enters his home.

Inside, he picks up a shearing knife from a shelf and goes back to the window. The shutter is closed tightly, but there is a small hole in the bottom to look through. The cold air seeping in makes him blink a few times.

He can only see part of the meadow. He moves to another shutter and looks out again.

The man is still standing there. He did not imagine it. *Danger.*

But why would a bandit stand in the open to be seen? On a freezing night? It would not be worth any plunder at a poor farmhouse to take such a risk by himself.

A messenger? Then why wouldn't he come to the door, or call to Shamgar when he had been outside?

He decides that something more threatening needs to be in his hands before confronting the stranger. He walks to another corner of the room where his oxgoad is propped against the wall. He tucks the shearing knife in his robe and picks up the heavy herding tool.

He is glad he brought it in earlier that day to rewrap the grip with leather strips. It is as tall as he is and has a thick oakwood handle. The head, made of Philistine iron, is a sharp point with a curved hook beneath it. On the base of the handle is another iron tip. Such iron is very rare in these lands. It is his most valuable possession, a wedding gift from his father.

He returns to the door, lifts the latch, and goes outside.

❦   2   ❦

THE STRANGER IS STILL STANDING at the edge of the woods.

Shamgar watches him for a moment. Perhaps his eyes are playing tricks on him and it is a stump catching the light. No—he knows this meadow perfectly. Nothing is there.

He gathers his courage and crosses the meadow towards the man, holding his head erect and the oxgoad in front of him with both hands.

"Who are you?" he asks.

The stranger is wearing a traveling cloak. His face is covered in the shadow of his hood. He holds a shepherd's staff.

"Tell me who you are," Shamgar demands. He stops a few paces in front of the man.

"Will you invite me in on this cold night?"

The stranger's voice is calm. Shamgar has to shout to be heard over the wind, but the stranger does not. It seems as if his words dart between the gusts, finding perfect clarity.

"I would need your name first," Shamgar says.

"It is impolite to ask, son of Abraham."

"You are mistaken. I am not an Israelite."

"I am not mistaken."

Shamgar frowns.

"My family is inside and I will defend them with my life. State your business here."

"Your family is in danger, but not from me."

Shamgar is about to raise his voice. Then an odd thing happens.

The wind dies down suddenly. The trees stop swaying. The snow ceases blowing through the meadow.

Shamgar looks around. He slowly lifts the oxgoad, his knuckles straining on the grip.

"Would you invite me in?" the man asks again.

Shamgar hesitates. It feels dangerous here, but something else, too. He cannot discern it. He finds himself nodding.

The man makes his way towards the house. Shamgar stays behind him as they cross the meadow. When they reach the door, the wind suddenly returns. Shamgar looks up the pass and sees snow clouds forming in the distance.

WHEN HE ENTERS, the stranger walks to the corner of the room and stands still. He never lets go of his shepherd's staff

"Can I take your cloak?" Shamgar asks quietly.

"I will not be here long."

Shamgar takes his seat by the fire and waits for him to say something.

"The sign was in the sky," the stranger says.

"The blood moon?"

"That is what you call it, yes."

"It has been years."

"Philistines are coming."

"They normally do in the spring. Bands of them take livestock or crops from us."

"They are marching through the pass and will be in the Boundary of Blood today."

Shamgar sits forward in bewilderment. "The pass? They

always come through the valley below Azekah. And it is still winter, how can they navigate our mountains?"

"They have been preparing. They know Ehud son of Gera is dead and your people are leaderless."

"Why do you call them my people? I am the son of Anath, a Canaanite."

"They will violate every woman and they will take the children as slaves."

Shamgar feels like laughing at this absurdity, but the stranger has no mirth on his face.

"The men?"

"The men will be left to plant crops and herd livestock, and all will be surrendered to Philistia at harvest."

Shamgar is unsure of what to say. Thinks about the nightmares he has been having.

"Why now?"

For the first time, the stranger smiles.

"Yahweh has chosen you to stand against them."

"The Hebrew god? Not even Hebrews believe in him."

"He has chosen you."

"Me?"

The stranger nods.

Shamgar tries to hide his confusion. He asks, "Why does he not choose a Hebrew?"

"Yahweh's people have lost heart, and have whored themselves out to the gods of the land. Even so, he will deliver them, because he is faithful when they are not."

Shamgar waits awhile to respond. He shakes his head and laughs.

"How am I to believe this? I am not a warrior."

The stranger's smile is gone now, and Shamgar senses that he has offended him.

"Go to the boundary and meet the enemy, and you will prevail."

A noise in the corner of the room. Shamgar turns and sees his wife is standing in the doorway to their bedroom.

"Why are you still awake?" she asks.

"We have a guest."

Shamgar turns to introduce the stranger, but the man is gone.

HE STARES A MOMENT. Then he stands up and walks to the door. His wife wraps her blanket tighter.

"What are you talking about?" she asks through her yawn.

"Did you see him leave?"

"Who?"

Shamgar opens the door and steps outside.

The snowstorm is coming quickly up the valley. The wind is raging. Blowing snow obscures the edge of the woods.

He looks down for any footprints. There are none. No sign of anyone.

"What are you doing?" his wife asks.

"He was here!"

"Who?"

"The man!"

"What man? Come inside."

Shamgar shivers against the wind. He looks up. The moon is behind the clouds.

"Come inside!"

He gestures for her to be quiet. Straining his eyes, he searches the meadow. Then he walks around the house looking for tracks. Still nothing.

Returning to his front door, he glances around again once more before going inside.

"Have you lost your mind?" She wraps a blanket around his shoulders. "What is going on? What is this about a man?"

Shamgar sits down next to the fireplace.

"Did you hear me speaking?" he asks.

CHAPTER 2

"What?"

"Is that what woke you? Did you hear me speaking?"

"Yes."

"So you heard the other man?"

"I only heard you. What happened?" She kneels at his feet and wraps his wet legs with the blanket.

"There was a man with me in this room."

"Perhaps it was a dream."

"No, he was here. I met him in the meadow under the blood moon and invited him inside, and he was here in the room with me when you entered. Then he was gone."

"A blood moon? What do—"

"There was a blood moon outside!"

She stops rubbing his legs and holds her finger up to quiet him. He can see her fight to keep her tone respectful.

"Shamgar," she says under her breath, "we were sleeping. I woke up because I heard your voice."

Shamgar looks at the fire. Tries to concentrate, but all is vague.

"You have been laboring for many days," she continues. "You are exhausted."

"I am certain he was here."

"What did he look like?"

"He was . . . " Shamgar considers it. "Something odd about him."

"Did he give you his name? Where he is from?"

"No."

"Come to bed."

"I need to think for a while."

"You need to get your rest before going to see Zebulun tomorrow. Come back to bed."

"I believe we are in danger."

"We are always in danger. Bandits are everywhere."

"This is different. I saw him. He was here. He warned me."

"Warned you about what?"

Shamgar tells her what the man said, and as he does, her expression changes from concern to anger. When he finishes, she looks away.

"Are you trying to hide from Zebulun?"

"Did you hear what I said? Philistines are coming."

"It is winter!"

"But . . . the blood moon was there. That is their sign."

"There are no Philistines. Are you trying to hide from him?"

Shamgar squeezes the arms of his chair to control his temper. "I am not trying to hide from him."

"He is demanding his payment this week. We will lose everything if you do not persuade—"

"*I know this!*"

It comes out louder than he wants. His wife sits back and wipes the corner of her eyes. Then she rises and walks to the fireplace.

"It is close enough to morning anyway. I will start preparing the meal," she says.

Shamgar watches her work. After a while he stands and says, "I will leave to see him now."

"Don't go out now! It is very early, and the storm is—"

"I will wait outside his house," he says, picking up his cloak.

"You should wait," she says, but he leaves without another word.

$\maltese$ 3 $\maltese$

SHAMGAR WALKS through the meadow in front of his house. Dense clouds have filled the pass, and the wind is unrelenting. It feels like snow is about to fall.

He reaches the forest and tries to quicken his pace, but the ground under the snow is uneven and slippery. Several times he slips and collapses. It normally takes an hour to walk to town, but it will take him longer today in these conditions.

Was the man real?

Philistines in the pass? A blood moon?

It could all have been imagined. He is very tired. Not been sleeping well.

There is a shepherd's shelter nearby for use when sudden storms flash through the mountains and strand men tending their flocks. He decides to wait there until the sun rises.

The shelter is nestled deep in the woods and cannot be seen by travelers on the trade road. It is small; only intended to be enough for one man. A small pen for sheep is nearby. Only a poor man's flock can fit inside of it. Shamgar built the shelter and sheep pen with other men in the valley several years ago after a boy was caught in a snowstorm and froze to death, along with his family's herd.

When he walks in, he lights the lamp with his flint and sits down on the mat. Thinks about lighting a fire in the hearth as well but decides against it. Too tired.

For a while he sits and stares at the floor, unable to decide what to do next. Escape with his family? They could never return to their home. And the shame it would bring to his father's name is unbearable.

He feels his eyes getting heavy and lets himself lay down on a wool blanket . . .

. . . and he is there with the stranger in the meadow under the blood moon, the eerie glow making it look like the earth itself is bleeding, and the forest black in the blood shadows, and the stranger watches him, waits for him to speak . . . but he *cannot speak*, cannot ask his questions, for the night is cold and his words do not come.

The stranger glares at him . . . demands to know why he has delayed . . . and then the figure transforms, the cloak melting away into fiery armor fastened to a warrior, terrible rage flowing from him as he commands Shamgar to answer . . .

SHAMGAR WAKES up in deep terror. Sweat drenches him. He kicks away the wool blanket. Sees dim morning light seeping in under the door. It takes him a moment to remember where he is. Realizes he has been asleep for several hours because it is fully light now. He holds his breath and listens. All he hears is the wind.

Snow is falling outside. It will be a miserable journey to Azekah. Surely his task can wait another day. He is angry. Angry at having another strange dream. And yet, this one felt . . . different.

"Should I go to the city?" he asks himself in the quiet room. Perhaps this god Yahweh will answer him aloud. He waits half-heartedly, knowing there will be no answer. The

Hebrew god is invisible, the elders say. He no longer speaks with men.

Shamgar decides to return home and come back another day. Perhaps Zebulun truly did forget about him. He can return later and find out.

Before leaving, he looks around the shack to see if anything needs to be resupplied. The firewood is stacked, the blankets are dry.

He chooses his steps carefully as he walks. After a while he turns at the place where the path to his farm begins. Out of habit, he inspects each piece of fence as he passes through the woods. The wooden fence planks are rotten in many places. Much work to be done replacing them in the spring.

Soon his house is in view. He walks to the barn and checks on the livestock. His pair of oxen are standing in their pen lazily chewing hay. The hens cluck as they hunt for grain left over from when he tossed feed the day before. Nothing amiss.

He leaves the barn and walks the short distance to his front door, kicking off the snow from his boots before entering.

Inside, his children are helping their mother clean ashes out of the fireplace.

"It is snowing again," his son says as Shamgar hangs his cloak on the nail.

"I noticed when I was walking through it," Shamgar says playfully.

"Mama said you should have eaten before leaving," his daughter says.

"Yes she did. I should listen to her, shouldn't I?" He tussles the girl's hair as he takes his seat.

His wife brings him a bowl of stew and he takes several bites. She sits down at his feet and asks him softly, "What are your thoughts?"

"I do not know."

"Did you go to Zebulun?"

"No."

"Where have you been?"

"I needed some time to think."

She frowns at him.

"I don't understand. Are you hoping he forgets the debt?"

Shamgar takes another bite, then sets the bowl down. Watches his son sweeping ash into a bucket with the broom.

"Of course he will not forget it."

"What do you want to do?" his wife asks.

"I think we are in danger. From Philistines."

She sighs and lowers her head. Turns to the children and says, "We need to get more wood inside before snow covers all of it. And check on the animals when you pass the barn."

They get up and gather their cloaks.

"Where are my boots?" his son asks.

"Where did you have them last?"

"Here. I took them off here."

When the children are finally dressed and gone, his wife paces near him with her arms crossed.

"I know it was a mistake to take silver from him," he says.

She does not look at him as she walks over and starts preparing flour.

"I told you I regret it. I will work forever to repay it if I have to."

"You should have listened to me," she says.

"How many times will you need to say this?"

"Our children will suffer for what you did. They will be poor their entire lives."

"That is ridiculous."

She finishes scraping the ground wheat into a bowl and wipes her eyes with a rag.

He feels a thousand things ready to burst from his tongue. How they had discussed the transaction, and how it was a good opportunity to finally own their land, and how, for once, he would be a respected man in the valley.

But these things have been said. Many times.

Shamgar decides he needs to leave before he says anything hateful. He stands up, hands her his bowl, and walks to his cloak.

"I am going to see Zebulun."

"Don't go back out, you are—"

"I want this finished!"

He says it angrily enough that she knows to stay quiet. He walks outside, too upset to put on his cloak in the house.

As he crosses the field he sees his children emerging from the barn.

"Are the animals well?"

"Yes, father," his son says.

"I will return later."

He trudges into the woods. He wants to be angry with his wife, but he knows she has done nothing wrong. Shamgar wants to be angry with Zebulun, but he, too, did nothing wrong. The fault lies entirely with him.

He shakes his head. A Philistine invasion.

Nonsense.

THE PATH IS EASIER to walk since he has already trodden down the snow, and he makes better time back into the pass.

Nearby is a well that the women of the valley previously used to fetch water. It was a peaceful place away from the towns where they could gossip and socialize, where arrangements were made for helping during the harvests, where they plotted marriages for their children.

Now, his wife and children are never permitted to leave their homestead without him, not for any reason. The attacks from bandits have been unrelenting. No road in the land is safe.

When he reaches the trade road he pauses and looks around the valley of Elah. To his right, the valley narrows as it climbs eastward up into the mountains.

To his left, the valley bends north before returning to its

westerly path. Overlooking this bend on a hilltop is the city of Azekah. Beyond that, the valley broadens until it reaches the Philistine cities in the coastlands.

The valley of Elah is the most direct route to Hebrew lands and the valuable trade roads to Damascus, and it is where the Philistines always travel when they wish to show their power over the Israelites.

In Joshua's time, Azekah was built to guard the valley and its vital access to the interior. If it falls, then only one place remains to stop an enemy—the place where he now stands. Cliffs tower on either side of him, small trees and brush tenaciously clinging to their sides. They call it the Boundary of Blood.

Shamgar looks at the ground beneath him. Snow covers most of it, but a few stones remain visible.

The legends speak of old days when men chose a rock in this place to make their stand, commanded to spill their blood over it in death rather than let the enemy advance. A narrow road traverses the pass south of here and ends at the boundary in the valley, known only to those who dwell in the region. This is where the stranger told him to go.

But there are no Philistines in sight, and Shamgar wonders if he has lost his mind as well as his heart. Besides, Azekah might as well be a trading post instead of a fortified city protecting the land. Long gone are the days when the men who reside there would be willing to resist an enemy.

$$\text{❋}\quad 4 \quad\text{❋}$$

SHAMGAR CONTINUES west through the valley.

In spring and summer this is a place of grazing for the animals owned by the men of Azekah. Their shepherds fiercely guard the springs and streams from anyone seeking refreshment. More than once, Shamgar has had to track a missing goat into this part of the valley and confront them. It never ends peacefully. Azekah is full of cruel men. Zebulun among them.

Soon he is ascending the road to the city wall. It looms over him from its place on top of the ridge, where, on a clear day, one could see nearly the entire region.

As he nears the gate house of the city watch, a watchman steps out and says, "Terrible day to be traveling, friend! Name and purpose?"

"Shamgar, son of Anath. I am here to speak with the elder Zebulun."

"You chose a fine time for it, storms all around and freezing cold. He is expecting you?"

"Yes."

The watchman walks back to the gate and opens the wicket entrance. As Shamgar approaches it, he asks, "Was there a blood moon last night? I awoke and thought it might have been."

The watchman frowns. "I never heard a report of one. The men on the third watch would have said something."

"Have you seen anything strange in the valley? Anything coming from the west?"

"The clouds are low and it is hard to see very far. A few travelers here and there. We saw you coming from a distance, but there was no one else around you."

Shamgar nods. "Thank you, friend."

Ducking his head, Shamgar steps through the gate and into the town of Azekah.

On normal days this is a hectic, bustling place. Vendors shout and haggle, animals bleat and moan, children shout as they play. Hundreds of people crowd into the small courtyard where the elders sit on stools, conducting their business and greeting important men who come through the gates.

Today it is nearly empty. The only other person he sees is a woman drawing water for her pitcher from a cistern.

Shamgar lingers in the courtyard. Wind swirls the falling snow, building it up in doorways and along the alley walls.

Go to Zebulun about his debts?

Try to warn the other elders?

He cannot decide what to do.

The woman at the well finishes filling her pitcher and departs the cistern. He thinks about approaching her, but it would be very strange and would only serve to frighten her. Right before she disappears from sight, he decides to follow her. She makes her way down a small alley and opens a door to what appears to be an inn.

He hurries to catch the door before she shuts it, startling her. She is wrapped in heavy cloaks and only her eyes are visible.

He bows his head slightly.

"I need shelter."

～

THE DEN SMELLS of aromatic spices and incense. A fire crackles in the fireplace, casting a warm, flickering glow across the room. Several young women sit in front of it, their hands busy with sewing as they chat happily.

Shamgar steps inside, the scent and warmth enveloping him. As he begins removing his cloak, two of the women stand and approach him. One, a beautiful girl with a red shawl, smiles and says, "Why are you out on such a day? Let me take your cloak." He nods, his gaze lingering on her as she gently takes the garment from his hands.

"I assumed there would be no visitors today," says the woman he followed from the well. She removes her own cloak, revealing herself to be around his age, her hair adorned with intricate braids and rings in her ears and nose. She must be the innkeeper, he thinks—a good place to start in a city when one is looking for powerful men.

"My apologies for frightening you," Shamgar says, his voice steady but low.

She smiles at him, handing her own cloak to one of the girls. "I saw you come through the gate. I should have asked if you needed a place to stay."

"I need to find town elders to speak with. It is urgent."

"On a day like today? Is something wrong?"

Shamgar hesitates, feeling foolish. Wonders again why he has come.

"Important matters. It is urgent."

"I am afraid no one will see you in these conditions."

"Can you tell me where their homes are?"

"Arrive unexpected at their homes? Then they are sure to listen to you." She says this playfully, and Shamgar looks at the floor with embarrassment.

"I apologize for inconveniencing you."

She steps closer. "It is no inconvenience, sir. Would you share your name?"

"I prefer not."

"I recognize you. You must live nearby. I see you in the market."

"I will take my cloak now, please."

She walks to the corner of the room, taking her time. As she slowly returns with his cloak, Shamgar notices the two younger women moving in behind him, subtly blocking his way to the door. He realizes at last what this place is and feels even more foolish.

"You can stay here and wait for the storm to pass. Half the price since it is a slow day," the innkeeper says.

"I need to find the elders. It is urgent."

"Tell me and perhaps I can help."

The one with the red shawl touches his wrist, her fingers warm and soft.

It is time to leave, he knows. And yet . . . surely, staying a few hours would not matter. Or a night. All is lost anyway.

Philistines are in the boundary.

He turns to see who said it, but the only ones present are the women. He feels the room grow still.

And yet, he heard it—the distinct emergence of a voice. Looks around again. No one there.

He finally pulls his hand away from her and reaches for his cloak.

"There is danger coming," he tells the innkeeper.

The innkeeper seems to want to laugh at this, but she restrains herself.

"Who is coming?"

"Philistines."

"Philistines always come here."

"An . . . army of them is coming to enslave the valley and take this town."

"You saw them?"

"No."

"Then how do you know?"

How is he supposed to answer? He had a vision? A dream?

"Did you see the blood moon last night?"

She laughs. "None of us are on the watch. How would we know?"

That teasing smile emerges from her again as she watches him struggle to reply.

"Philistines bring me good business," she says.

"They will destroy everything this time."

"Why do you believe this if you did not see them?"

"I was warned."

"Warned by who?"

She waits for his answer, the younger women edging closer.

It is all madness. No reason for him to continue on with this foolishness about false warnings of imaginary Philistines. He can wait here, then go home tomorrow. Tell his wife the storm trapped him.

Sensing his resolve weakening, she says, "A third the price. My final offer. You can have the one from Ammon."

She nods at the girl in the red shawl, who presses her hand onto his lower back and leans in. He smells the perfumed oil on her. Feels her hair brush against his sleeve.

Philistines are in the boundary.

He turns sharply, searching the room.

"What is wrong?" the innkeeper asks.

"There is no one else here?"

"There is no one."

Shamgar watches them. Then he slowly pulls the cloak from her hands.

"I am grateful for the offer, but I must leave," he says.

"We will be here," she says with another smile, opening the door for him.

❅ 5 ❅

OUTSIDE, Shamgar inhales a long, steady breath.

To get to Zebulun's house he must go back through the courtyard. He makes his way across it, stepping carefully around the snowdrifts. A few merchants have opened their booths, though no customers seem likely to appear.

The house is at the top of a narrow, steep alley. His boots slip on the ice-covered paving stones as he ascends it, using his oxgoad for balance. Finally, he arrives at a wide door in the center of a high wall.

Five years ago. That was when he stood at this door and waited to see this man about a loan.

He takes another long breath to gather his courage and pulls the bell string.

Soon, the door opens and a slave girl looks out at him.

"My name is Shamgar son of Anath, and I have business with your master Zebulun."

"My master is not seeing anyone today," she says, and starts closing the door.

"Please. I owe him money. He will want to see me."

She hesitates, then nods. "Wait here." She closes the door.

He looks around. Two men walk up the alley towards him,

wrapped tightly against the cold, their breath visible in the frosty air. They move quickly, heads down, as if eager to escape the chill. No one else stirs in the deserted street, the silence broken only by the occasional howl of a wind gust.

He feels his chin drop until it rests on his chest.

So very tired . . .

Try not to slouch so much, his wife always tells him.

He straightens up, forcing his shoulders back and lifting his head. The cold bites at his exposed skin.

The two men pass by without a glance, their footsteps fading in the distance. Shamgar breathes deeply, feeling the crisp air fill his lungs. He flexes his fingers, trying to keep them from going numb, and shifts his weight from one foot to the other.

The city feels . . . strange. Normally there is life everywhere, even in winter. Especially in winter, because people have more time for leisure since the harvest is in.

A stray dog trots past, sniffing at the ground, its fur matted and dirty. It glances at Shamgar with wary eyes before scurrying away. He watches it disappear around a corner, then returns his gaze to the empty alley.

He thinks of his wife again, and the children.

NEARLY AN HOUR PASSES as Shamgar stands at the door. His anger and frustration at being treated this way build. But what can he do about it? The man inside this house owns him now.

The door opens at last, and the slave girl gestures for him to follow her, latching the door closed behind them. He leans his oxgoad next to the door frame and waits for his eyes to adjust to the dark. When he is ready, the slave girl leads him down a corridor.

They eventually come to a room with several windows, all opened and letting in the cold wind and dreary light. An enormously fat man with a thick gray beard is laying on cushions next to a dining spread. Despite the chill in the room, Zebulun dabs the sweat from his forehead with a cloth. His wealth is evident in the abundance of food and the luxurious cushions that barely contain his sprawling form. The room smells of roasted meat and spices, a stark contrast to the outside world.

"Farmer. I did not expect you to come to me. I was ready to send collecting officers from the town. You have all of it?"

"My lord, I only have a hundred."

Zebulun reaches over and grabs a piece of lamb from his plate, grease smearing his fingers. "That is a tenth of what you owe to me."

"Part of the crop failed this year, and Philistines and Amalekites raided the rest. My oxen went lame. I could not hire out."

"How are you going to pay it?" Zebulun asks, barely looking at him as he chews noisily.

"I will work for you, lord."

Zebulun reaches over for another piece of meat. "I have enough workers," he says.

"My oxen along with me."

"How old are the animals?"

"Ten years."

Zebulun chuckles.

"Only one hundred, and a pair of old oxen. Ridiculous. How long have you been in my debt?"

"Five years, lord."

Zebulun dips a piece of bread into olive oil and takes a bite. He studies Shamgar as he chews.

"I will take your children into my household for five years."

Shamgar feels something churn deep in his chest. His legs grow weak.

"Lord, please. I beg for more time."

"I have already given you time."

"Please, I beg you, lord." Shamgar kneels down and puts his head on the ground. The grit of the floor presses into his forehead. He searches for something, anything to say. "Please, lord. One more season."

Zebulun takes another bite, wiping oil from his chin. "Bring them to me by tomorrow, or I will have you and your wife sold as well."

Shamgar keeps his forehead pressed against the ice-cold paving stone. "Please. I will do—"

"Do what? I have rights to everything you own. Be grateful I am letting you keep your feeble oxen."

Zebulun claps his hands together and the slave girl appears.

Shamgar slowly rises. Looks at the girl more closely. Probably in her twelfth or thirteenth year. A debt paid by another family.

"Lord . . . please . . . "

"Out."

As Shamgar leaves he sees several other children in the house, all busy with chores, their faces blank with resignation. No adult servants anywhere. At the doorway, he takes his oxgoad and walks outside.

HE STEADIES himself with one hand on the wall of the house. The wind whips down the alley into his face. No part of him seems to work. His chest is numb. His legs shaking.

He takes a step down the alley and slips on a patch of ice, landing hard on his side. Laying there a moment, he wonders if he should get up. It is cold enough to freeze to death. All he needs to do is wait until nightfall.

No, someone would report him.

He gets up slowly, his hip sore from the fall.

After half-walking, half-sliding down the street, he reaches the courtyard again. More people are here now than earlier, but still only a few. Servants are brushing snow from doorways.

He passes a mother and her children holding their cloaks up against the wind as they leave the cistern. Passes a stall where a butcher holds out a quarter of lamb to him, which he waves away. The city gate is ahead.

The pain begins to emerge from deep within. A pain in what feels like his very soul. Desperate to numb it, he finds himself turning down the street to the inn.

❧   6   ❧

THE FIREPLACE IS ROARING BRIGHTLY with freshly-piled wood, and this time the air is thick with fragrant myrrh—something he has smelled only a few times in his life. The warmth and scent wrap around him, making his head swim.

A servant girl appears next to him, silently taking his cloak, her touch soft and lingering more than necessary. The innkeeper enters from another room, her eyes glittering in the firelight. She says she is glad to see him again, but his ears are ringing, and her words sound hollow, as if coming from a far distance.

"Where is the one with the red shawl?" he demands, his voice husky.

The innkeeper tilts her head slowly. "The Ammonite. I thought you might like her. She is expensive."

"I will pay it."

"I heard you owe a great amount of silver to Zebulun." She says it flirtatiously, but he feels a surge of embarrassment, unsure how to reply.

She touches his waist, then runs her fingers up his arm.

"I inquired when you left. I know everything in my city."

The weariness comes again. He knows what he looks like to this woman. A pathetic, desperate man. He hates being poor, hates being mocked. Hates the woman in front of him with her gently scornful eyes. She sees the truth about us all, he thinks as he looks at her painted lips. The truth about every man.

"Bring her out."

The innkeeper smiles, waiting. He realizes she wants to see the money first. He reaches up and pats the pocket of his cloak. The coins clink together deep in the folds. His anger surprises him, but he does not restrain it. "Do you frequently humiliate your customers?"

She steps back and bows her head respectfully. "Forgive me, sir. There are some who want the service and carry nothing with them. You understand."

She gives him another coy smile as she departs the room.

Two young women enter and recline on couches. They stare directly at him. Their gazes feel like physical touches, their boldness unsettling, and he is unsure what to do. No woman is so forward as to stare at a man, yet here is a place where they all do it.

He looks around the room. Drapes of thick colored fabric over the windows. Cushions on every chair and reclining couch. Platters of dried dates and nuts. This is a place for the upper men; the men who reign and rule.

The innkeeper returns with the red shawl woman. More of a girl than a woman, he decides. Her hair is curled and flowing down her shoulders. Jewelry on every finger, rings in her ears. Painted eyes.

She walks confidently up to him and takes him by the elbow. Her touch is light.

Then . . .

A glance, just for an instant. Her eyes revealing something.

Disdain. Scorn. Fear. All of those things in a single look.

"Come sir," the girl says, all smiling pleasure now. But he cannot make himself go with her. He saw what he saw. He steps back, gingerly taking her hand away from his arm.

Philistines are in the boundary.

CHAPTER 6

"They are not in the boundary!" he says, turning around.

No one is there.

The room is quiet as they watch him.

"I am sorry to have bothered you," he mutters, and steps backwards, reaching for the door latch.

"What is wrong?" the innkeeper asks him.

"I must be going, I am late."

"You will pay for this girl!" the innkeeper snaps at him, and he sees, finally, her pure disdain, part of her face in shadow, part of it in firelight.

"I took nothing, I owe nothing. Give me my cloak or I will notify the watch."

The innkeeper laughs.

"The watch? The chief watchman is my customer. You wish to complain to him?"

Shamgar hesitates. The others in the room watch him in the humiliating silence.

This must cost him something. It is what he deserves.

He fumbles into his pouch, pulls out a handful of shekels, and hands them to the innkeeper.

"For touching her. And for wasting your time."

The innkeeper's smile returns, warmer than ever.

"You are certain you wish to leave? We enjoy these games with you."

§ 7 §

SHAMGAR THINKS about their mocking eyes as he crosses the courtyard, and he thinks about the voice, certain he is losing his mind. When he arrives at the city gate the watchman approaches.

"Did you have your business with Zebulun?"

"I did."

"Your name? I need it for the records."

"Shamgar. I told you earlier."

The watchman raises his hands.

"Apologies, friend. A lot of people come and go from here."

"Forgive me. It has been a long day."

A smile returns to the watchman's face. "It is only the noon hour. I pray that Yahweh will bless the rest of your day."

"You are a Yahweh worshipper?"

"He is the God of our people."

Shamgar shakes his head. "No one seems to worship him."

"Few worship him, it is true. But he did not become less worthy of it. If one man in the city can be faithful to him, perhaps he will give his blessings to us."

Shamgar frowns. This is the first mention of Yahweh he has

heard in a long time, apart from what the stranger told him last night.

"Do you need anything else, friend?" the watchman asks, smiling at him again. It is genuine. Shamgar feels warmth for the first time this day.

"No . . . thank you, though."

The watchman opens the wicket gate for him and he walks through it.

The snow is not falling. A small mercy. But the wind is miserable and the walk home will be long. He follows the tracks in the snow that he made earlier.

The clouds are too low to see far today, but he can see the boundary, and there are still no Philistines in it.

It comes into his mind, with crushing certainty, that he is about to surrender his children in slavery to Zebulun. This makes him slow down, then stop.

How is he supposed to breathe? His throat feels constricted, like powerful hands are wrapped around it. A burning in his chest.

Philistines are in the boundary.

"Stop! Enough!" he yells, turning to look in every direction. "There are no Philistines in the boundary! Look for yourself!"

All he sees is the dark forest, and the empty road into the valley ahead. He is alone.

"Why do you torment me?" he says, quieter now, speaking to no one.

He wonders if his own father imagined things at the end of his life. He was not a man who spoke often. Never would have told Shamgar anything of the sort. But still, he wonders.

He descends from Azekah and makes his way into the valley. The wind howls, the bits of ice sting, and he does not care anymore because he is thinking about home.

Home—where he will tell his wife that their children are now slaves because of his debts.

Death can be found in the cold streambed nearby. He could lay in it and soak his cloak, then crawl into the snow. Freezing is like falling asleep. He will not feel it for long.

He finds himself drifting to his left where the creek is. Standing on the bank, he sees that ice has formed on the edges, but water is still flowing. All he needs to do is lay down in it.

Philistines are in the boundary.

This time he does not startle. He remains still. Listening. It is not an actual voice, as though a man were standing next to him speaking words. It is . . . what? What is it?

He listens a moment longer, but nothing further comes. Finds himself stepping back from the creek bank, then turning away from it.

Soon he walks into the boundary. The cliffs on either side of the trade road block the wind and he lets his cloak drop away from his face, his breath coming out in frosted bursts. The road itself, normally muddy in winter, has frozen into jagged ruts covered in ice.

He looks at the boulder-strewn passage into the mountains and laughs to himself. Laughs about choosing a blood rock, and the absurdity of it all.

WHEN HE REACHES his meadow he turns into the barn. The oxen are still calm. The hens peck for grain among the hay stalks.

He puts some more grain on the ground for the hens and leaves the barn. Unable to delay further, he walks into his house.

His wife is stirring a pot of the afternoon meal. His children are playing a game in the corner. He feels very, very tired . . .

"Were you able to speak with him?" his wife asks, looking up.

Shamgar nods. She waits for him to elaborate, but he only sits down next to the fire in his chair.

To his son and daughter, he says, "Go to the barn for a while so I can speak with your mother."

His tone is firm enough that they offer no protest. When the door shuts behind them, Shamgar slouches further into his chair.

"He is demanding the children."

A deep silence comes into the room. His wife kneels down where she is and starts to quietly weep.

"When?" she finally asks.

"Tomorrow."

He sits forward and rubs his eyes with his fingers.

"We must pack and leave today. We will go south and I will find labor there. It will be planting season soon in the south. We leave after we eat."

Now he musters the courage to look at her. She stares back at him. Not with anger, but with something much worse: shame.

As they pack their belongings, his confused children ask him many questions. He lies at first, telling them they are only moving south for more work, but they are old enough to realize leaving so abruptly is suspicious.

"We cannot stay," he finally says, "if we do, they will take you from us."

"Why will they take us?"

"Because we owe silver to a powerful man."

He says this many times and they hear it every time, but still they ask. His wife does nothing to silence them, letting him feel the deepest parts of his failure.

Finally he is unable to bear it and retreats to the barn.

Placing the harnesses on the oxen, he feels completely lost. He stops moving and watches the snow lightly blowing through the window shutter.

Where are they even supposed to go?
Philistines are in the boundary.
"Stop!" he yells. To no one.

🙣   8   🙥

SHAMGAR HITCHES the oxen to the cart and takes them outside. His wife and children carry belongings from the house and start filling it up. He goes back inside and searches for his own things that will make the journey.

He sees his wife coming through the entrance and stands aside for her. Waits for her to raise her eyes to him even once. She does not.

It takes his family an hour to gather what they can carry. Food for a week. Blankets and winter clothing. Cookware. Each child has their favorite plaything.

His son is crying loudly as he says goodbye to the hens. He loves the silly birds. His daughter is quiet, like her mother.

The last thing Shamgar takes is the oxgoad. He had a bronze sickle blade for years until it finally shattered last summer when he struck a rock during a lazy moment harvesting wheat. No money to have it fixed. This is all he has left, and it will need to serve as a weapon for the road.

Much danger lies ahead of them. Such easy prey for bandits —one man with an attractive woman and two young children. If they make it three days without being captured and sold to slavers, it will surprise him.

He looks at his family. His son watches him. His wife and daughter stand quietly waiting, staring at the ground.

"We will return," he says as confidently as he can. This makes his wife finally glance at him, but her glare makes him turn away.

Shamgar looks over his home a final time. The parts he inherited from his father, the parts he built himself. He glances at the edge of the clearing. Was it only last night that he saw the vision of the man? His world undone in a single day.

He jabs the goad into the lead ox's hide and the team starts moving, grateful that the snow is not too deep to travel through with the cart.

He wonders how far they can get before dark. At least five hours travel; far enough to get out of the snow into the lower elevations. They will travel down the Elah valley and take the interior road south to Judah. A tent is in the ox cart; his family can live in it for as long as necessary if someone will lend them the land to pitch it on.

He has healthy oxen. This will save them. Few common men have such an advantage. He will offer himself and his team of oxen to the first farmer who could use his help. They are prosperous in Judah; close to Egyptian markets and able to sell excess grain to traders.

They reach the valley road and he stops to adjust the harness on the animals.

"You may get in the cart now, I will stay on the ground to lead them," he tells his family, and his wife helps the children crawl onto the back before climbing up herself.

He pulls a blanket over them.

"Thank you," his daughter says. She is the only one speaking with him now.

"Stay warm, little dove, we will not travel far today."

She nods at him. He feels the edge of his eyes start to burn with tears.

Back to the front, he prods the oxen left and onto the westward road. The oxen shake their heads and give a low rumble of displeasure at the added weight.

"*Tch tch*, easy," he says as he pats them on the heads.

The clouds hover on the tops of the mountains. The wind is steady but the snow has held off.

When in despair, find one thing to be grateful for.

His father's words. So be it.

"I am grateful that the snow has not fallen again and made this passage more difficult," he mutters to himself.

He takes several more steps and sees a snowflake, then another. The backs of his oxen are soon covered.

There it is. The gods faithfully providing discouragement at the time of greatest need.

He has tears, and since no one can see him, he lets them fall down his beard, freezing into ice as he walks. He does not bother to wipe them away.

They travel around the bend, then another. The snow is falling very hard now and the oxen are struggling to gain footing.

"They might break a leg," his wife says from the cart. It is the first thing she has said since he told them they were leaving. She is correct; the oxen cannot be risked. He stops their movement.

Shamgar looks around them for any type of shelter. Not far away the forest reaches the valley floor in a gap between the steep slopes. He blinks away the snow as he studies it. A few of the smaller trees are bent over, forming an overhead shelter of boughs. Not much, but it is the only choice they have.

He looks at his wife. She is watching him from under the blanket. Still no anger. Only disdain.

"We will wait over there," he says. She tilts her head slightly and shrugs.

Shamgar prods the oxen into turning off the road, then moves to the front so he can check the ground. He remembers this area; it is a flat, grassy field in the summer months. As long as there are no hidden sinkholes, they should make it.

Step after step he guides them. Once, the supporting animal

stumbles into the leader and they both nearly fall, but the leader holds strong and manages to keep them up. Shamgar pats him on the neck.

When the oxen reach the trees, he has them pull the cart through a narrow opening between the trunks. It is a good spot to wait out the weather. He can get the tent out, string it between the cart and the trees, and form a warm shelter.

With his family out of the cart, he tells his son to build the fire and his daughter to help him with the ropes. His wife holds one end of the animal canvas as he pulls it taut over the edge of the cart. Wrapping it back around, he creates a tent shelter. The animals will not be exposed either; the trees are thick enough to shield them.

Inside, his son has constructed a strong fire using wood stored in the cart. He reaches up to clear the ceiling vent from tree boughs outside to let the smoke drift out.

When all is settled, they sit close together and listen to the wind.

"How far from home are we?" his daughter asks.

"Not far," he says. "A hour's walk."

"Then why are we here?"

"We cannot go home, little dove. We must not be anywhere near it."

"Not even for the storm?"

Shamgar takes a moment to respond. They could have waited in their home and left the next morning. Zebulun would not have sent men that quickly. He is waiting for Shamgar to bring the children to him. They had time. Why rush out in such a panic? Can he not make a single wise decision?

"Better to get it over with," his wife says. "We would need to leave tomorrow anyway, and they would have a better chance of catching us."

"Why are we leaving?"

His daughter keeps asking this and it frustrates him. How many times must he be forced to—

"Because your father borrowed silver from a man he should not have borrowed from, in spite of me warning him, and now the time has ended for him to repay it. The man has demanded you and your brother as payment. We cannot let that happen."

"Why couldn't you find silver to pay the man?" his daughter asks after a moment.

Shamgar looks down. Finally manages to answer, "I tried."

His wife opens her mouth to say something else. Shamgar braces for it, but nothing comes. In the dim light of the tent he sees her staring at him. He knows her very well; she has restrained her tongue for the sake of the children.

❧ *9* ❧

THE WIND BLOWS ALL EVENING, and the snow gathers around their tent. His wife passes around bread for a meal and melts snow for water. Soon, they are asleep under their blankets.

Shamgar watches the flames until they fade into coals. Sleep feels like a mistake. He will only wake up again, and the torment will resume.

As snowfall patters against the tent, he feels his mind slipping. Finds himself thinking of the dancing at their wedding, with tambourines ringing and beads clattering as the virgins of the valley twirled around them, his father beaming with pride next to her father, his brothers teasing him. Her laughter. Twenty years she has been his companion. Children lost, many hardships endured together. Thinks of the night disease killed their son. The day disease took their daughter. Holding her through it all.

Deep love that grew over time.

Gone, now.

He feels so very, very weary . . . slowly falls asleep . . .

~

First, he feels a cold darkness. Then a gray light emerges, like twilight, and he finds himself standing on the edge of a vast sea.

Far away are mountains; higher than any he has known. A fleck of sunlight sits on the jagged peaks. The azure sky above is clear; not a cloud in sight

A soft wind comes from the sea, carrying the faint scent of salt, and distant pine. The surface of the water ripples gently; no waves roll in. It is eerily calm, almost as if the sea is holding its breath. He looks down and realizes he is not on a shoreline at all, but standing on the water itself. His feet are just below the surface, solid ground beneath them, but land is far away—a distant promise.

When he musters the courage to turn his head, he sees that the mountains surround the entire sea, enclosing the earth.

And then he sees the man.

The stranger from the woods stands there, wearing armor of astonishing beauty, intricate designs shimmering in the dim light. His eyes are fixed on Shamgar's, intense and unwavering, as if they hold the weight of ages.

Shamgar feels his breath catch, his chest tight with awe and fear. He notices a large basin in front of the man, appearing to be made of bronze, its surface glowing warmly. Inside, a fire blazes, the flames swirling and dancing as though alive.

The stranger speaks . . . and his voice roars, powerful and deep, like it could threaten the stars above . . .

Shamgar wakes up to a cold tent. His family is still asleep under their blanket. Snow and ice no longer pelt the roof. Dim morning light slips between the gaps of their shelter.

He is afraid. Unable to even move from this fear.

It was only a dream . . . yet it was real. And the voice? The voice that has been haunting him . . .

Philistines are in the boundary, and your delay offends Him.

Slowly, he pulls out a few pieces of kindling and strikes the flint.

The fire lit, Shamgar drapes his blanket over the children and crawls through the flaps.

Calm outside. A fresh layer of snow covers the cart. If he did not know it was there, it would be hard to spot.

The oxen are gone.

He panics. Tries to remember if he tied them. He was so tired, so distraught, he might have forgotten.

He searches the snow frantically for their tracks but the drifts have covered any sign of them. He grabs the oxgoad from the cart and stumbles wildly out of the trees.

The pass is calm. Storm clouds hover on the peaks. Shamgar staggers forward through deep snow, desperate to find the oxen before his wife wakes up and there is even more to blame him for.

This angers him. Why should he even care what she thinks?

He reaches the road and looks east and west. It takes him a moment to notice that the snow has been freshly trampled. At first he thinks it is the oxen, but it has been packed down from human footfalls, not hooves.

Someone is standing in the distance.

Nothing strange about this; it is a well-traveled highway and Azekah is the most important town in the valley. As Shamgar continues, he sees that the man is now kneeling down. He appears to be studying something on the ground.

"Greetings," he says as he gets closer, "I am looking for a team of oxen."

With his back turned, the man continues his work, oblivious to Shamgar's approach. Shamgar circles to get a better view, but before he can close the distance, the figure stands and turns, exposing his face under the hood.

It is a woman.

She stares directly at him. He can see her eyes as she studies his movements. She has tattoos on her forehead and face. He notices, now, that her cloak is more of a temple robe than a traveling garment; deep green and black, and stitched with patterns of Philistine gods—he recognizes Dagon, but not the other one. It looks like a goddess. But who?

"Do you need help?" Shamgar asks. A woman alone on the roads is unheard of, Philistine or not.

Movement to his left. Now he sees that she is *not* alone.

A man emerges from behind a tree. He is a Philistine soldier with full armor, an iron spear in one hand and iron sword in the other. His helmet has a facial guard on it, and black horsehair sticks up at its crest. The breastplate of his armor is forged with great skill; this is obvious even from a distance.

More men emerge out of the forest. At least twelve of them, dressed the same as the first one.

Shamgar backs away. He bows his head submissively.

"My apologies," he says in Philistine. He knows some phrases and words, but he hopes they do not require him to speak more of their tongue.

The woman watches him a moment. Then she steps slowly aside and reveals what she has been doing.

Blood fills the snow around the body of a young girl. He sees a deep cut on her neck where the woman has slashed it.

Shamgar feels something churn in his gut. He takes a step back.

"The first virgin," the woman utters.

Surprise crosses her countenance, then is quickly gone. She keeps her eyes fixed on him.

"What are you doing?" he manages to say.

The woman raises her arm, her bloody wrist holding a bloody dagger. She releases the weapon and it falls point-first into the snow.

She speaks in the Israelite tongue now, in a sensual low voice, and somehow this frightens him more than anything yet.

"Our army will not move past this place until your god has shown himself. Tell the men of Azekah to send their champion, and we will see whose god controls these lands. If no one comes, we will burn every man, woman, and child alive in this valley as a sacrifice to Ashtoreth."

Shamgar takes a few steps backwards. He resists the urge to look towards his family at the oxcart.

She smiles at him. Turns her gaze to where his family waits, then back to him.

"Hurry along, farmer. Azekah has one day to send their man."

She turns and walks away. The Philistine soldiers follow her, leering at him as they leave.

Shamgar can do nothing but stand and watch for a long moment. Then he staggers forward and kneels next to the girl. She is still warm; the killing happened a short while ago.

He touches her neck where the dagger slashed it. Young, soft skin. She is a Hebrew, by her garments, and appears to be in her eighth or ninth year. The same age as his daughter.

The woman is a long distance away now. The soldiers are behind her in an orderly column. He takes a few steps after them. Then he stops.

What does he think he can do? Attack them all himself?

But that was what the warrior told him to do.

Unless he is imagining this. Imagining all of it.

He wipes his wet face with the back of his hand. Looks down the valley.

They are disappearing around the bend.

Philistines kill Hebrews. It happens all the time. It is not his affair, not his business.

Shamgar looks back at the dead girl. Wind rushes up the valley and sprays his face with snow and ice again. It howls, rages, much worse than before. He raises his cloak to ward it off. When it calms for a moment, he sees that the Philistines are gone.

This shakes him out of his confusion. He needs to get his family and escape the valley. He starts running, then stops again.

The woman said they have one day to answer the summons.

This will be his reason to summon the elders. No more false blood moons. He can shout and pound on doors and do whatever it takes to get their attention. A murdered Hebrew girl and a troop of Philistines is worth rousing them from their firesides. Perhaps the city elders will be grateful for the warning, and force Zebulun to give him more time.

And the stranger. His command to stand in the pass. What if it is real? That Yahweh will use him?

It is time to be brave, Shamgar decides. For once in his life.

Philistines are in the Boundary of Blood.

❧ 10 ❧

WHEN HE GETS to the cart, he pulls aside the tent flap. His wife is warming bread on a stone next to the fire, his children sitting under their blankets waiting for it.

"The oxen are missing," his wife says curtly.

"We need to move now." He grabs the blankets from the children, who groan in protest.

"What is the hurry?" his wife asks. "What is going on? Where are the oxen?"

"The Philistines are coming. We must warn the city."

His wife has been getting to her feet to help him. Now she stops.

"I saw them," he continues, "we must get to the city before they come."

"Tell me what you saw."

"Do what I say!"

She turns, resigned, and starts picking up bags of food and water.

"Where are the oxen?" his wife asks again.

"They got loose in the storm, I don't know."

"How are we supposed to pull—"

"Stop arguing with me!" Shamgar yells. It is so loud, so

violent, that the children draw back to their mother, terror on their faces.

She pulls them close to her.

"You are scaring them!"

Shamgar stops moving. Takes a long, slow breath. Decides he needs another one and takes it, too.

"I saw them. It was exactly as the warrior told me."

His wife looks down. It is a long moment before she speaks again.

"How *dare* you speak of visions—"

"It was not a vision!"

"—and how *dare* you frighten our children, and lose our oxen—"

"They escaped, I thought I tied them."

"—and *how dare you lose our home!*"

He has no answer.

Her sobbing erupts from a deep place within her. "We will be disgraced forever. My father shamed! Our children have to carry your name, and you have shamed them! *You have shamed them!*"

The last part comes out as a wail, not a shout, and she drops to her knees, the sobs no longer controlled. She weeps into the sleeve of his son.

"You ruined us," she says between the gasps. "And now you would take them right to the city where they will be enslaved because *you are a coward.*"

Gone are her attempts at being respectful for the sake of the children. Now it is all before them. All under the sun. Everything said.

They stand as a family in the forest, tears on the children's faces. Tears on his wife's face. There is nothing he can do but drop to his knees. All of his strength has dissipated.

Slowly, he says, "We need to leave. The cart is well hidden. We can return later and get it."

She seems to gather herself. "What about the oxen?"

"I will find the oxen later."

"At least take us back to our home. Force Zebulun to come and get them."

His mind is inflamed at her obstinance. But what else could she be expected to say? What else could she think?

"If I can show you that they are coming, and that we are in danger, will you follow me?"

The glare eases the slightest bit. She takes a quivering breath.

She wipes her eyes quickly and stands up. "Very well. Children, we need to go." She puts the pack over her shoulder. "We will follow."

He looks for something in her eyes. Anything. She gives him nothing.

He turns and leads them out of the woods.

SHAMGAR KEEPS some distance between himself and his children, not wanting them to see what is ahead. As soon as he can make out the girl's body on the road, he kneels down in front of his daughter to block her view.

"My dove, I need you to stay here with your brother while I show your mother something."

She pulls back from him slightly. He sees fear in her—remembers he just yelled at her like she was an enemy.

"Do you forgive me for shouting? I did not mean to frighten you."

She nods. Relaxes a bit.

He looks at his son. "Can you protect your sister a moment? We will be back quickly."

The boy nods. Shamgar gestures for his wife to follow him.

As they walk, Shamgar says, "Prepare yourself. It is a terrible thing."

She does not respond.

When they are close enough, he holds his hand up to point.

His wife looks up and then lets out a gasp, putting her hand over her mouth.

So much blood has drained from her corpse that her flesh has a gray pallor, and a dark stain surrounds her on the ice. A light layer of snow covers her garments and her hair, giving her a ghostly appearance.

"Oh . . . God of my people," his wife mutters.

Shamgar tells her quickly about the woman, the soldiers, and the instructions for Israel to send its champion by tomorrow. His wife listens without looking away from the dead girl.

"She said her goddess was testing the Hebrew god, to see if he controls the boundary into Israelite lands," he continues. "They will burn every home and village in the valley."

His wife approaches the body slowly and leans over it. "It is Azariah's daughter!"

Another farmer in the pass. A good man; Azariah and Shamgar occasionally help one another with tools and labor. Shamgar puts his hand out to his wife, and this time she turns and buries her face in his chest. He holds her tightly.

"Tell me again what he told you. The man who came to you."

With these words from her, it feels like a yoke has fallen from his neck. He is no longer alone.

"He said Philistines were going to come through the boundary . . . " He hesitates. "And that Yahweh, the Hebrew god, was commanding me to save his people."

"You?"

"It makes no sense to me, either."

"You believe this message?"

"I do not know."

She puts her head on his shoulder.

"I am sorry for doubting what you told me," she says.

"You had every reason to doubt me."

Shamgar lets go of her and kneels down. He brushes snow onto the corpse of the girl to hide her from view.

"Stay here and wait for me to bring the children past."

He walks back through the drifts to his daughter and picks her up. His son steps in his footprints as they walk.

His wife is kneeling down near the corpse, blocking the view.

"What is wrong, mama?" his daughter asks.

"I am fixing my sandal," his wife says, smiling. "I will be right behind."

Shamgar passes her and leads his family onto the boundary road.

❧ II ❧

SHAMGAR'S DAUGHTER holds his neck tightly as they ascend the hill to the city gate. His wife pulls along their son by the hand.

The watchman emerges from the gatehouse and holds up his hands.

"I see you brought the family this time," he says, smiling warmly.

"Please, we need to warn the city."

"Warn the city about what?"

"Philistines are coming."

The watchman chuckles. "Philistines always come through."

"They are coming to burn the city."

The watchman waits for a smile or a laugh.

"I am not teasing. Please, let us in. A girl is dead. I need to see the elders. Truly."

The watchman sees their expressions and his smile fades.

"You know where to find them?"

"I know where Zebulun lives. He can lead me to the others."

The watchman looks at the oxgoad.

"The only weapon I have," Shamgar says.

The watchman opens the wicket entrance and Shamgar leads his family through.

They hurry across the courtyard and turn past the entrance to the inn. Shamgar, afraid of being recognized, hopes one of the innkeeper's women is not out in the streets, but the city is quiet. The market vendors who opened earlier must have changed their minds.

He climbs up the alley to Zebulun's house. Ice on the stones makes it a slow walk. When they finally reach his door, he pounds on it with the oxgoad.

The same slave girl from earlier answers. As soon as she sees him, she opens the door wider. "My lord is in counsel with the other elders."

"Here?"

"No, sir."

"Tell me where."

"I cannot, sir."

His wife steps closer. "Please, dear one, tell us. What we have to tell him is very important."

"He gave very strict instructions. He is not to be disturbed. I am sorry."

She starts to close the door.

"Please!" Shamgar says, sliding his hand into the doorway to block it. "This is life and death. Life and death."

"I am sorry, sir, I cannot—"

Shamgar suddenly grabs her by the throat and shoves his way through the door, pinning her against the wall. She gags, terror in her eyes.

"Tell me now or I vow by your god I will kill you here."

"Shamgar!" His wife tries to pull his arm away. His daughter, whom he is still holding in his other arm, cries and struggles against him.

The slave girl tries to nod and Shamgar eases his grip.

The slave girl holds her throat, her face lowered in fright. "There is a council room in the square. They convened an hour ago."

Shamgar turns and hurries down the alley. He puts his

daughter down and pulls her along, occasionally sliding on the ice until he reaches the bottom.

"You did not have to threaten that girl!" his wife says behind him.

"There is no more time."

"You need to calm down," she says, though her own voice is agitated. He reaches out to steady her. She wipes away another tear.

"Where do you want us to stay?" she finally says.

He curses to himself as he remembers that she and the children cannot enter a counsel. They could be stoned on sight.

"Is there no one in the city we can go to?"

He shakes his head. Most of the men he knew in the city either died or left years ago.

He knocks on the nearest door. A woman opens it, listens briefly to his story, and closes the door before he finishes speaking. He does this at several more homes, frantically beating on all of them, until someone yells that they are summoning the watch if he does not stop.

Shamgar leads his family back to the courtyard. None of the vendors are willing to help them, either. He is threatened again with the watch, and this gives him sudden hope that he knows where to go.

"Can my family stay in your shelter?" Shamgar calls out to the gatehouse as they draw near.

The watchman emerges and shakes his head. "I am sorry my friend, but no one can stay in it. For any reason. Those are the commands."

"Only for a bit until I can speak to the elders."

"I am sorry. We are asked all the time by travelers and it has been forbidden."

"Please!"

"They will be safe in the courtyard."

"But it is freezing out here!"

His wife touches his arm. "We will find a place. You must hurry."

Shamgar looks around angrily. People around the courtyard only stare back at him, unwilling to help a desperate man.

"Is the the council room still down that alley?" he asks the watchman.

"Yes."

"I will be back soon," Shamgar says to his children. "Do exactly as your mother says."

HE KNOWS where the council room is because he once had to settle a dispute with a neighboring farmer. Another failure in his life, he thinks bitterly.

When he gets to the door, he takes a moment to calm himself down, because Zebulun will be inside. He will be the impossible one to convince, will turn the others from even listening to him.

"Hebrew God, if you are there, this is the time to begin helping me," he mutters under his breath, and pushes the door open.

LANTERNS LIGHT THE ENTRY HALL. Two servants stand near the door and seem startled Shamgar did not knock. Across the hall he sees a room with men seated, lit by several windows on the walls above them. One of them is talking, then stops.

"Who is there? What is this?" the speaker yells.

Shamgar hands his oxgoad to one of the servants, who takes it in bewilderment, and walks into the chamber.

"Lords, forgive my intrusion, but Philistines are invading. They have given a challenge of the gods."

The men in the room look around at each other.

"Who are you? What do you mean invasion?" the speaker asks.

"This man is a farmer in the pass near the boundary," comes a familiar voice, and Shamgar closes his eyes to steady himself. "He owes me his children as payment on a loan, and it appears he is trying to distract from that."

"Lord, I saw them."

"Who?"

"Philistines. They killed a girl from the valley and are gathering an army to come to the city. They are giving Azekah until nightfall to send their champion."

Zebulun rises from his seat. He walks toward Shamgar, his posture erect so his belly protrudes through his cloak. Shamgar has a sudden urge to ram the tip of the oxgoad into Zebulun's gut.

"We could stone you for interrupting us," Zebulun says.

"That will not change anything. They are coming."

"Philistines, you say."

"Yes!"

Zebulun stares at him casually. He turns and walks in front of the council seats. "This man owes me a thousand shekels of silver. He says he cannot pay it, so I am claiming his children as debtor's rights."

There is murmuring among a few of the men in the room. Shamgar feels his temper rising.

"My debts are not why I am here. You must all warn the city and help me stop them."

This leads to laughter in the room. Zebulun paces around Shamgar, his breathing heavy with effort. He dabs his sweating forehead with a cloth. Shamgar tries not to look at him.

"Where is this girl?"

An older man in the corner is the one who asks this, and Shamgar turns to him in relief.

"The Boundary of Blood. They are provoking Yahweh."

The old man stands, slowly, and makes his way to the floor. Everyone waits respectfully.

Shamgar finally recognizes him. His name is Meshullam and he was at the city gates for business once when Shamgar visited. Meshullam is near his sixtieth year, and has scars from disease on his neck and face. One of his eyes is clouded, and he needs to tilt his head to be able to look at something. He holds power in this room because other men have not contested the conversation.

"I am Meshullam, the son of Ira," he says when he reaches the center of the room.

"We met once, lord," Shamgar says.

"You are speaking the truth?"

"I vow it, lord."

"He is lying. How would they have marched past the city without being seen by our watchman?" Zebulun says.

"Perhaps the weather hid them," Meshullam answers.

Shamgar looks around at them. "I am a ruined man. But I am not lying about this. All I ask is that someone come and see the girl. Test what I say."

"Whose son did you say you were?" asks Meshullam.

"I am the son of Anath, a farmer in the pass for forty years."

"I knew of him. Honorable man."

"Thank you, lord."

Zebulun scoffs at this and picks up his cane. "I will remove him from the room and we can continue our business. Does anyone dispute my right to his children as servants?"

The men look at one another and seem to settle back in.

Shamgar tries to keep his voice calm, but feels his desperation growing.

"Lords, I do not dispute this man's claim to my children. That is not why I am here. Indeed, I was fleeing from Zebulun this very morning."

This causes more commotion. Zebulun grins at him and walks closer. His belly is near Shamgar's waist. Shamgar has never wanted to strike a man more in his life.

"See? He admits to fleeing a debt. His wife is now forfeit to me as well."

"And yet, he did not actually flee," says Meshullam, tilting his head to see Shamgar with his good eye. "The man risks much coming here and admitting this. We ought to investigate his claims."

Zebulun dabs his forehead and chuckles. "You will go out on a day like this? Why would an army from the plains ever come in winter? Why would they be coming at all?"

Shamgar knows the answers to all of these questions and starts to speak. Then he remembers it was told to him *in a vision,* and he needs to be careful.

He says, "They could be coming into the boundary on the forest road from the south, and I believe they have a new goddess. The woman I saw appeared to be a witch or a priestess, but not from Dagon. She said the name 'Ashtoreth.'"

Meshullam has been pacing slowly around the room. He pauses. "The south? That road is far too long for them to use from the plains, and they would not know how to follow it."

"Lord, they are determined to destroy us. Parading in front of our city straight up the valley would have given us warning. They could already be between Azekah and the rest of the Israelite lands. All that stops them now is the god-challenge."

Zebulun starts to protest again but Meshullam raises his hand. "A new goddess, you say?" he asks.

"Yes, lord."

Meshullam turns to the room. "Does anyone else wish to speak?"

A few voices raise, but one shout is heard above them.

"I have heard of this goddess!"

Shamgar turns and sees Nahor son of Anaiah rising from his seat. He feels deep relief; he has known Nahor a long time.

"I did not know you were in this counsel, Nahor."

"I inherited the seat from my father," Nahor says, smiling at him.

"When did he die?"

"Last year."

Shamgar bows slightly. "He was a good man."

"I would have spoken up in your defense earlier. When Meshullam stood, it would have been against our protocol until he was finished." Nahor turns to the others. "I will accompany the farmer to the boundary and verify what he claims. I can speak for this man's character. He might owe many debts, and I do not dispute Zebulun's claim on his children if he himself does not, but if Shamgar son of Anath says a god-challenge has been issued and Philistines are coming, we must listen. And, yes, I have heard that a new goddess has influence over the Philistine kings."

This causes more commotion. Meshullam holds his hands up to quiet them and looks at Shamgar.

"With Ehud dead, we no longer have a champion in all of Israel, much less this city," Meshullam says.

Nahor places his hand on Shamgar's shoulder.

"I say again that I will accompany Shamgar to the boundary. If what he says is true, it is a terrible emergency. If it is not, he can turn over his children to Zebulun this very day. Is that agreeable to all?"

"You swear before these men that this is not an attempt to hide your debts?" Meshullam asks.

"I swear it on my father's honorable name."

"If Nahor accompanies him, then this is worthy of our time to consider."

There are nods all around. Zebulun raises his hands and shakes them to give his begrudging assent.

NAHOR GUIDES SHAMGAR OUT of the room. Shamgar takes his oxgoad from the servant at the door before stepping outside. Nahor pulls his cloak up to his neck against the wind.

"You chose a fine day to disrupt our honorable gathering. We weren't going to meet until after the weather passed, but Zebulun wanted a decision on a tax at the gate before the next caravan arrives," Nahor says.

Shamgar realizes that Nahor does not believe him. "Philistines are coming, Nahor."

Nahor smiles grimly at him and lowers his voice. "I understand your desperation, friend. I can help you escape with your family."

"There will be no escape for any of us. They are coming."

Nahor shifts on his feet. "We have known one another a long time. Our fathers before that. You do not need to lead me on like the others. I will make it seem like you had no choice but to—"

"Nahor, listen to me! They are coming! You must see this girl's body!"

Nahor lifts his palms and steps back.

"I did not mean to offend you."

Shamgar shakes his head. "I am sorry. I have not slept well in a long time." He continues walking. "You said you have heard of this Ashtoreth goddess?"

"She does not have her own temple yet, only dedicated followers. They say the King of Gath has her priestess on his council. She is called the Handmaiden of Ashtoreth."

"That must have been her I saw in the boundary."

He and Nahor enter the courtyard and Shamgar looks around for his family. Vendors and more townspeople are out, but he does not see them anywhere.

"My wife and children are here somewhere," he says.

"Did no one take them in?"

Shamgar shakes his head.

"The city used to be more welcoming. My father made certain of it," Nahor says.

Shamgar is about to return to the gate and ask the watchman when he notices the door of the inn nearby. He walks over to it.

Nahor looks around. "Do you know what this place is?"

"Yes, and the women here know more about what happens in this town than anyone."

Shamgar knocks on the door, trying to hide his nerves from Nahor. Soon it opens and reveals the innkeeper. She appears to be expecting him by the way she smiles.

"Did you see a family in the courtyard?" he asks her before she can speak. "They were seeking shelter. A woman and two children. I am trying to find them."

"We are here," comes the voice of his wife, and he sees her standing behind the innkeeper.

❧ 13 ❧

At first, Shamgar can only stare at his wife. He feels something hollow in his chest as he rests the oxgoad on the entry post.

But the innkeeper's smile is warm.

"When I saw them in the courtyard I was worried and brought them in. She has been telling me about the Philistines," she says. "I told her you stopped here yesterday seeking shelter before returning home."

"Thank you for letting them stay here," Shamgar says. The woman nods politely. He sees something in her eyes. *Your secret is safe.* Shame washes over him.

"What have the elders decided?" she asks.

"I will accompany Shamgar to the boundary, then return and give a report to the elders. If this is genuine, we will decide what to do," Nahor says.

"It is genuine," Shamgar says sharply. "An Israelite will need to fight their champion." He hesitates. "Can my family stay here until I return?" he asks the innkeeper.

"Yes, if they help prepare the evening meal for travelers who arrived earlier."

"This is the safest place for you while I am gone," Shamgar

says to his wife. She nods and embraces him. He kneels down and hugs his children tightly.

Shamgar follows Nahor to the door, where the innkeeper has opened it for them. He picks up the oxgoad from the entry post, and as he leaves, he feels the innkeeper watching him.

SHAMGAR AND NAHOR make their way across the courtyard.

"If I had known you were here, your family could have stayed at my house. You can bring them now if you wish." Nahor says.

"I am grateful for your offer, but they need something to occupy them while I am gone."

At the gate, the watchman opens the wicket to let them through.

"We will be back shortly," Shamgar tells him.

"Did they listen to you?"

"Not yet. Nahor is coming to verify it."

The watchman bows to him respectfully.

Shamgar thinks about it and asks, "Can you come as well?"

The watchman looks up at the sky. "More weather is coming."

"This is very important. We need more witnesses."

"Let me speak with the commander."

The watchman returns to his gatehouse and then reemerges with an older man, who appears annoyed that his afternoon rest has been disturbed.

"What is this about Philistines?"

Nahor says, "There is a dead Hebrew girl in the boundary. This farmer says she was killed by a Philistine priestess as a god-challenge, and that an invasion force is coming from the south through the Boundary of Blood."

The watch commander offers no immediate response. He calmly looks from Nahor to Shamgar, then back to Nahor.

"That is quite a lot."

"Yes," Nahor says, and Shamgar notices a slight curl at the edge of his mouth. Nahor still does not believe him; this saddens more than angers him.

But the watch commander does not mock him. Instead, he says, "You are prepared to swear this? If you are lying you will be tied to the post and whipped for spreading a false threat."

"I swear it by every god," Shamgar says.

The old man nods. "How far away?"

"An hour's walk. Half if we hurry."

The watch commander turns to the watchman. "This could be nothing, but to be safe, have the men on the wall pace the routes faster, and tell the reserves to be ready. I will be back in several hours."

The watchman bows and holds the wicket open. Gathering his cloak and sword, the watch commander steps through the gate, followed by Nahor and Shamgar.

As they descend the road towards the valley floor, Shamgar recounts for the watch commander all that has happened, leaving out the stranger and the visions. When he is finished, the watch commander says, "What was she wearing?"

"A green robe."

"Be more specific. Describe it."

Shamgar concentrates on his memories.

"It had silver weaves in it. Like a pattern. Dagon and a goddess."

"Never heard of it," the watch commander answers. "I suppose they do find new gods and goddesses frequently down on the plains."

Nahor tries to walk closer to him but Shamgar is too angry to speak with the man. The sooner he can show them the corpse, the better.

The way is clear ahead. A high cloud ceiling but no snow falling yet. After an hour, they turn the corner in the valley and ascend the narrow pass at the edge of the Boundary of Blood.

"In the old days we had a watch posted here," the watch

commander says. "Best place to defend against invasion in the valley, and you could guard against someone coming from the south through this road. A hundred hard men can stop thousands. Gath itself could not get through here in all their hordes." He points to a spot nearby. "My blood rock is there."

"Mine is further down. I wanted to get my death over with quickly should it come to that," Nahor says.

The men laugh at this and Shamgar feels his anger dissipating. Nahor is a good man. If more good men appear, it could be done.

~

A LIGHT LAYER of snowfall covers the girl, but the pool of her blood is still stark against the white.

Nahor and the watch commander walk up to her silently. The watch commander kneels and brushes off some of the snow.

"You knew the girl?" he asks.

"I know her father," Shamgar answers.

Nahor seems stunned. Shamgar waits for him to say something. A long moment passes.

The watch commander says, "Did anyone witness the killing besides you?"

Shamgar shakes his head.

The watch commander sighs. "It will be difficult proving that it was Philistines who did this. What do you say, lord?"

Nahor does not respond—he is looking behind them.

They emerge; first dozens, then hundreds, an endless snake of a formation stretching down the road. The air grows thick with the sound of their boots pounding the earth, a rhythmic thunder that reverberates through the valley.

Armor glints in the pale light, each soldier clad in dark iron, casting shadows on the snow. Banners flutter in the wind, emblazoned with the fearsome symbols of their gods.

The ground seems to tremble under their weight. The

clinking of weapons, and guttural commands barked in a harsh tongue. Spears and swords gleam in the winter light. The sheer number of them is overwhelming, a relentless tide of death and conquest, each step bringing them closer to their prey.

All three men understand that the worst has happened: the Philistines have bypassed the valley and marched through the mountains, and now they are fortifying the Boundary of Blood.

"I . . . apologize for doubting you," Nahor says.

PART II

We come now, my king, to the arrival of Philistines in the Boundary of Blood.

You must be wondering, as Shamgar did, why they choose to invade now?

The existence of a new goddess coming to power in those days is true and based on records we have acquired from Philistia. And, indeed, she was called the Ashtoreth. Her influence spread during the later years of Ehud, pulling many important officials and rulers into her sway. We know she demanded the sacrifice of children and the growth of temple prostitution, promising that the land would be fertile and flush like the swollen belly of a pregnant woman.

But what led to this moment, this very hour, where an entire army marched in winter?

One month prior to Shamgar's visit from the stranger, there was a gathering . . .

$$\textbf{\maltese} \quad 14 \quad \textbf{\maltese}$$

THE TEMPLE of Dagon wears night like a cloak. Shadows drape over its stone facade, muting its contours in the starlight and making the towering columns seem like they were carved by giants.

The air is thick with the mingled scents of incense and smoke, hinting at the sacrifices offered within. Priests tend the building every hour, and murmurs of their chants drift through the corridors, a low, unsettling hum of reverence. This is a place where darkness feels at home, where the walls seem to absorb the light, and every step echoes with the weight of ancient rituals. Here, in the temple of the horrible god of the sea, the night is a constant companion, and shadows hold their secrets close.

A servant stands in the entrance. He holds a torch over his head to light an oil lamp, and when it sparks to life he stands back and watches it a moment. When he is sure it will stay lit, he walks to the other door post and lights the next one.

Finished with the lamps, he takes his position near the entrance on a small bench in the alcove. He sits on the bench and eagerly unpacks the meal pouch his wife made for him. It is the best part of his shift, when he stands the overnight watch alone. The temple sacrifices are performed during the day, and that is when crowds and noise are abusive to his senses, his nostrils filled with the brine of rotting salt-wood, and the stench of animal slaughter.

He is senior to the other servants. He could demand the day, but he enjoys the night. Night is relief from the heat. Night is quiet. Nothing happens.

He opens his food pouch. Freshly baked bread, a dip of oil, a tear of pork. His favorite.

From his alcove he can see the entire harbor. Every ship leaving Philistia to challenge the sea routes gathers here in Ashkelon for their blessings. The sailors go in to the prostitutes, captains meet with their ship owners, incense is burned, animals sacrificed, and it is all a horde of misery in the day.

But night? Night is different. Night is when he can settle in and think about his remaining days. Ten more years until his servitude is over. He will be in his fortieth year. Old for some in his lands, but he is eating well and knows how to avoid the plagues. Perhaps the gods here will look favorably on him for his loyal, uncomplaining service.

His own gods surely see his faithfulness. He makes certain they are placed near his windows in his hut where they can see the city, and when he stands watch over the temple he brings them along. They are not majestic like Dagon, whose temple he serves in. They are small gods of the womb and the grain. They know their place and humble themselves before mighty Dagon of the sea.

His wife makes certain he never accidentally offends them, ensuring they are packed in his food pouch to be displayed in his alcove. In ten years, when he is free, he expects a reward from his gods. He expects them to plead for extra blessing from his masters. They will ask the majestic gods for additional sons to be born to him. He has seen such things happen to obedient men before.

He finishes his meal and settles in for his watch. There is a wool blanket under his bench. He pulls it out and wraps it around his shoulders. Winter rains have not fallen yet this week. A red sun that morning means they will be returning tomorrow.

In the west he already sees the clouds starting to form, blotting out the western stars. They will roll in from the sea and disrupt navigation plans, and tomorrow the temple will be filled with every mariner in the region beseeching Dagon to let them depart. It repeats itself every winter, then every summer, and time itself cannot change the cycle.

He smiles to himself. There is no changing the will of the gods. They will exert themselves on the earth. They will *force* obedience.

Ashkelon is a large city, spreading north and south along the coast of the Great Sea. Thousands of people, hundreds of homes, all crowded near the ports where the seafaring work is. Taverns, markets, teeming masses serving the god Dagon.

The temple is on a bank above the harbor. The only way up to it is a thin road that winds up the steep bluffs overlooking the sea, and it is on this road that he notices the figures.

He sits forward and squints his eyelids.

Three of them. Even from here he can make out the swiveling gait of two women, and what looks like a child walking between them.

He stands up and puts aside the food pouch, taking his fishtail staff and positioning himself in front of the entrance.

They wear hooded cloaks. Their steps are careful and feminine; no urgency as they approach.

When they reach the gate, he stands straight and holds out the staff.

"Our lord god Dagon demands your purpose here."

The three figures stop in front of him. The harbor twinkles in the moonlight behind them.

"You serve him well," one of the women says softly. Her face is in shadow and he cannot make it out.

The second woman moves slightly to his left. He is a trained man, a soldier and fighter, and he knows that such a movement is threatening under normal circumstances, but he is suddenly unable to get his mind to concentrate. The scent of myrrh drifts to his nostrils. He inhales it deeply, more than he should, and searches for words.

"Reveal your purpose," is all he can muster.

The woman in front of him moves closer. Darkness covers her, and she is careful to keep the moon behind her. He feels the second woman easing behind his arm, feels a slight brushing of her cloak against his elbow.

"Dagon sees your loyalty," the woman in front says.

He frowns at her. "Who are you to speak for Dagon? Step back."

She does not move. The other woman is now on his left, having circled behind him. Fool, he thinks. Letting her behind you without even an effort to stop her.

Myrrh and . . . lavender? Perhaps cinnamon? Extremely rare to smell these things. Only the slave girls in the harems of the king had such oils.

The woman in front of him says nothing for a long time. The other keeps circling. Again, he lets her pass behind him without stopping her. This time she brushes more of her body against his arm, slides behind him, and leans against his right arm.

He feels his breathing grow shallow.

Gods of the sea, *the scent* . . .

He swallows hard. "Remove your hood."

She reaches up slowly and pulls it down.

He sees long dark hair. The smooth skin of her neck and face in the moonlight. Tattoos on her forehead and at the corners of her lips. Her eyes are black like coals.

She tilts her head slightly and whispers, "Stand aside."

Cinnamon and myrrh. He is sure of it.

Then he realizes who they are.

"Mistress . . . I did not recognize you. My humblest apologies."

She smiles very slightly. "It is forgiven. We will have guests soon. Five of them with their servants. You will let them pass."

"Yes, mistress."

He feels his throat growing dry. Takes a hesitant step backwards. Both women watch him until he is back in his alcove. They walk past him to the door of the temple and slide their arms into the wicket. He hears the metallic clank of a lever being pulled, and the door swings open.

The black-eyed woman glances at him again before disappearing inside, the other one following her, leading the girl accompanying them.

~

THE TWO WOMEN, the Handmaiden and her acolyte, lead the girl down a long corridor, past the public halls and sacrificial pits, past the area for Dagon's priests, who watch them enviously.

They reach a door which opens into the chamber of the goddess.

Windows high above allow in thin moonlight. The women move quietly about the chamber, lighting oil lamps that cast a trembling glow and quivering shadows. Ornate carvings of pregnant sea creatures and fruit-filled vines cover the walls.

Towering into the dark is the goddess herself—towering, imposing, reaching to the ceiling high above.

The Handmaiden walks over to a corner and pulls a rope. A curtain withdraws from a skylight above them. She glances at the moon through the lower windows, then to the skylight again.

"One hour."

The acolyte kneels down and embraces the girl. "You are doing wonderfully," she says, "the goddess is pleased with you."

The girl nods at her, smiling, but her fear of this place is evident.

"Do you see the moon, my love?" the Handmaiden asks.

The girl nods.

"When it reaches the top," the Handmaiden points above her to the skylight, "she will be here, and she will give you the spirit." The Handmaiden kneels down in front of her until she is eye to eye. She holds the girl's face in her hands.

"Your bravery will be remembered, little sister," she says. "Now we must prepare."

The girl nods again. Fear in her eyes, yes, but also resolve.

The Handmaiden kisses her on the head.

OUTSIDE, the servant waits in terror.

He could not finish his meal, did not even return to it, and if he never eats again, he will not mind.

The Handmaiden of Ashtoreth. *Here*.

He studies the trail from the harbor as though it is his only purpose in life. When they come he must be ready.

He looks down at his idols.

"My lords, preserve me."

❧ 15 ☙

THE HANDMAIDEN OF ASHTORETH stands in the center of the room, staring at the moon overhead. She has pulled off the cloak and is now displaying her robes. Against the wall, towering to the ceiling, is her goddess.

Ashtoreth the elegant. Ashtoreth the mysterious. Ashtoreth of beauty and grace, and *power*. Her presence here known to all, but only the privileged can worship her. For now.

The Handmaiden looks at her again. She cannot help herself, her eyes forever drawn to worship. The curves of her legs, the delicacy of her hair.

The counter to Dagon's hardness. The completion.

The goddess wears a sea gown that roils across her waist and shoulders. The sculptor had been guided by the hands of Ashtoreth herself, it was known. Nothing else could explain the perfection of the lines, the harnessing of the deep black and pale white.

She deserves her own temple, and she will get one, deep inside the lands Dagon has never conquered.

The Handmaiden glances up. The moon is edging into the skylight.

"What will it feel like when the goddess comes?" asks the girl.

The Handmaiden walks to where she is laying on a stone table carved between the feet of the goddess. She runs her hands through the silky hair. Very soft. Prepared for days.

"It will feel like the most delicious sweet you have ever eaten. You love honey, yes?"

The girl nods.

"It is like honey spun from bees who live with the gods. It will warm you from the inside, as though a summer day visited you in winter."

The girl smiles. Her breathing is shaky. The Handmaiden continues to stroke her silky hair. Calm is essential. Calm is power.

"Are you afraid, my love?"

"A little."

"You must not be afraid. Do you feel safe with us?"

"Yes."

The Handmaiden smiles. Undying loyalty, for only a meal. The starving Hebrew family had been eager to release her. A year of grooming, a year of affection. A year of a full belly. The girl's first moon cycle has not come to her yet. No man has touched her. A month in the north for spices. A month in the south for oils. She is ready—if she is not afraid.

THE SERVANT HAS NOT MOVED for an hour, staring at the harbor trail.

Figures emerge at last. Five of them on horseback. He steps out and positions himself in front of the gate. He straightens his back as they approach him.

"My lords, they wait for you inside."

The one in front pauses a moment and looks around. He

nods his head at the others. They dismount and hand the reins to their servants.

"How long have they been here?" the leader asks.

"An hour, lord."

The man nods. The servant can see the corner of the man's robe slipping out beneath his riding cloak, confirming the rider's identity. He hurries over to the temple door and opens it, bowing as they walk inside.

When the last man has passed, he shuts the door, exhaling a long breath in relief.

THE FIVE KINGS of Philistia walk down the corridor until they are stopped by the acolyte standing in front of the chamber. Her robes of white fur sprawl across the stone. Her pale hair and paler skin seem to glow even in the darkness.

"The ceremony is not complete," she says.

"How much longer?" asks the King of Ashkelon.

"As long as it takes to read the sign."

"Do not speak in riddles, witch."

She watches him a moment. "As long as it takes to read the sign," she says again.

The King of Gath puts his hand on Ashkelon's shoulder. "We can wait in the council room."

The acolyte makes no movement as she watches them turn and walk down another hallway. When they are gone, she peers into the chamber.

The moon is in the skylight. The Handmaiden is kneeling next to the girl at the base of Ashtoreth but staring overhead.

"Bring them in," she says suddenly.

"I held them away."

"Bring them in!"

The acolyte bows her head and withdraws. She walks down

the corridor to the council room of the temple. As she enters, she sees that the kings have already taken their seats.

"You must come quickly, my lords. It is the sign."

Immediately they are on their feet and following her. She leads them into the chamber, where the Handmaiden is standing over the Hebrew girl with her arms raised. She has a dead hare in one hand and a knife in the other. The animal has been sliced open and its blood is dripping onto the Hebrew girl, whose eyes are closed in fright. The Handmaiden is muttering something to calm her.

The acolyte looks up.

The moon is in the skylight . . . but it is turning to blood. A blade of orange-red, shaped like a scimitar, is cutting slowly across it.

"The sign," she says.

The Handmaiden mutters an incantation. The acolyte sways gently. She hums the song prepared for this night. Quiet at first. Then louder. A song of harvest. A song of birth.

The blood moon is at half. Would a cloud pass over? A cloud would be Ashtoreth blocking the vision. The blood of the goddess's moon cycle must not be interrupted.

A moment of panic. She waits.

The crossing continues as the moon grows darker and redder until, at last, it is fully covered.

The Handmaiden raises her hands. She stares hard at the moon. The acolyte stops humming her song.

A flash of movement, only a moment, but it flickers across the sky in front of the red moon.

The Handmaiden releases her breath. She turns her gaze up to Ashtoreth. The goddess watches the sky.

"What is the sign?" the King of Gath asks.

The Handmaiden resumes stroking the Hebrew girl's hair.

"You must remain with us a while longer. Are you my brave girl?"

The girl nods her head. Her eyes search the woman's face, and the Handmaiden smiles warmly back at her.

"Your mother will be proud of you."

The girl nods again. A small grin.

The Handmaiden rises. She approaches the King of Gath. The acolyte draws close to her and places her hands on her robes. She kneels.

"Tell us the vision, my lady," she says.

The Handmaiden hesitates.

The acolyte searches her face for any meaning. This is unusual. Mother never hesitates. The gods must have spoken and the tiding is ill.

"The sign is complete," the Handmaiden says. "The blood moon is favorable for entering Israelite lands. Dagon comes from the sea. Ashtoreth is in the fields. Marduk resists, but Ashtoreth has persuaded him."

The King of Gath takes several steps into the chamber. He looks up. The room is still filled with blood-light.

"We will convene."

16

THE COUNCIL ROOM is dimly lit, with flickering oil lamps casting dancing shadows on the elegant furnishings. A fire pit in the center is surrounded by cushions where the five Philistine kings recline. Columns of the room are adorned with ornate carvings and tapestries depicting scenes of war and triumph. The aroma of incense permeates the room.

The Handmaiden slips into a shadow to observe the kings, and the acolyte does the same on the other side of the room.

"It is time," the Handmaiden says.

"You are certain?" the King of Ashkelon asks.

"She is certain," the acolyte responds.

"I saw it the same as the rest of you. The blood moon appeared precisely when they said it would. You cannot doubt anymore," the King of Gath says.

"Dagon has given the summer sign in winter. You anger him if you do not act," the Handmaiden says.

The King of Ashkelon looks around. "Any other words from the council?"

"I do not wish to anger Dagon," says the King of Ekron.

"There has never been a winter invasion. Why would the gods be commanding this now?"

CHAPTER 16

The Handmaiden is now moving around the kings, occasionally brushing against them and running her fingers along their shoulders. The acolyte does the same on the other side. All of the kings are transfixed by them—with the exception of the King of Ashkelon.

"Afraid of the cold weather, Ashkelon?" asks the King of Gath.

"I was leading armies when your mother conceived you. Do not speak to me of fear."

The King of Gath raises his hands respectfully. "A harmless jest. Apologies. Your counsel is wise, and I would not go against it myself, but the gods are speaking. You have seen it."

The King of Gaza adjusts himself on the cushions and says, "Marching an army through the mountains in winter might be foolish."

At this, the acolyte drifts toward the King of Gaza and stands very still behind him. Her fingers lightly stroke his back.

"But," he continues, "the blood moon in winter is undeniable."

"Can there be any other interpretation?" the King of Ashkelon asks wearily.

The Handmaiden has positioned herself behind him and is reaching out to touch his neck when Ashkelon brushes her aside.

Anger flares within her, and she almost loses herself. Almost.

"Dagon understands your concern. But he requires obedience to the wishes of his consort," she says.

Ashkelon ignores her, keeping his questions directed to the King of Gath.

"What is the route you plan to follow?"

Gath smiles. "We have an Israelite scout who can guide us through a southern pass into the valley. We will emerge behind Azekah and be deep within their lands before they realize it."

Ashkelon sighs. Looks around again.

"What about the Hebrew god?"

The King of Gath raises his hand to stop the Handmaiden from replying. "Legends and myths, Ashkelon."

"Legends and myths? Let me tell you one of the 'legends and myths.' There was a Hebrew warlord named Caleb who conquered the city of Kiriath-arba when he was eighty five years-old. Kiriath-arba was ruled by *Anakites*."

"Caleb is a myth created by the Hebrews to scare away weaker members of our race. Anakites are also myths. Our own giants are the sons of Dagon."

"Anakites are only myths now because Caleb killed them all."

A long silence in the room as Ashkelon turns his gaze from one to the other.

"What is an Anakite?" asks the King of Gaza.

"A half-man, half-demon. It is said they were twice as tall as normal men," replies Ashkelon.

"There is no reason to believe they were real," says Gath.

Ashkelon takes his time with his wine goblet before responding. He is the oldest man in the room, and his speaking is slow and methodical. Many years of wisdom accompany him in the council, whereas the younger kings are more impetuous and easily led. The Handmaiden hates all of them, but she hates Ashkelon most of all.

"My great grandfather was at Kiriath-arba. He was there for trade negotiations when Caleb attacked out of a storm, and was haunted the rest of his days by the sight of the old man slaughtering an army of Anakites. It was this memory that kept our city from ever attacking the Hebrews again. The only thing I can remember about my great grandfather is that story . . . and how terrified he was when he told it. He made my father vow not to attack the Hebrew lands when their god was present. My father passed that vow down to me."

The room is silent again. The Handmaiden is glaring at him, and the acolyte, seeing her, does the same.

"If this new goddess is as important as you say, I will not

interfere. But it must be your army, Gath, and you must accompany them. If you succeed, you will get the largest share."

He raises the goblet to his lips.

"But, if the Hebrew god awakens . . . "

He takes a long drink of his wine.

WHEN ALL OF the kings are gone, the King of Gath lingers in the chamber of the goddess.

The Handmaiden says, "We will issue the god-challenge when we arrive in the valley, and even the King of Ashkelon will know of her glorious triumph."

Gath looks at her. Her lips smiling, but her eyes black like shadows. It is said these women have them tattooed when they are girls to please the goddess.

"You have said all the correct things to persuade me, about trade routes and control of the hill country. Tell me, truly, what does Ashtoreth want in Hebrew lands?"

The Handmaiden looks up at the statue. Her smile widens.

"To destroy Azekah and every other Israelite city, and see her temples built on their ashes."

PART III

We never learned who the traitor was that led the Philistine army through the high country, but it does not matter. Every man in Israel in those days had lost heart. Perhaps the Philistines promised him bread for his family, or iron tools. Betrayal was easily purchased.

What matters for our story is that the King of Gath and the Hand-maiden of Ashtoreth have marched at the head of an army through the winding paths of the interior mountains, and now they are standing with their army east of the city, blocking the only escape route for the people.

❧ 17 ❧

NAHOR ARRIVES at the chamber before Shamgar. He swiftly removes his cloak and hands it off to a waiting servant as he enters the room. The elders are gathered, quietly conversing amongst themselves. A table has been prepared for them, and some are already seated around it.

"Philistines are in the valley," Nahor declares to the group. "Someone must have led them through a pass into the boundary behind us. We are cut off from the rest of the country."

This quiets everyone. Meshullam steps forward.

"How many?"

"Hundreds that we could see. Perhaps thousands."

The room erupts until Meshullam quiets them.

"Why don't they continue up the valley? They are already past us, why wait?"

"Ask your questions to Shamgar, whom you doubted," Nahor says angrily.

"They are waiting for a champion. We have until morning," Shamgar answers.

Zebulun, reclining in the corner, says, "The farmer may have killed her himself to fool all of you."

Shamgar is unable to restrain himself any further and rushes across the room to Zebulun, his fist raised to crush his face. The fat man's eyes grow wide and he struggles to get away. Shamgar grabs him by the front of his cloak as the room erupts with men shouting, "Stop!"

Shamgar pulls Zebulun's face close to his own, his fist raised, and says, "You already own all that I have. It will cost me nothing further to kill you."

Zebulun, shaking with fright, says, "Let go of me!"

"Enough!" Meshullam yells from across the room, loud enough to convince Shamgar to let go.

Zebulun drops back into his cushions. "This is outrageous!" he says.

"Close your mouth, Zebulun," Meshullam answers.

Zebulun reaches over and picks up a piece of bread. He wipes his forehead with his other hand. "We have no champion. You are all being foolish." He reaches over and picks up another piece of bread. "We should invite their king into the city and let him stay as our guest. He is obviously trying to impress the other Philistine kings. They will lose interest and move on soon enough."

"They will burn every farm in the valley, then burn this city," Shamgar says.

"Why would they do such a thing? They gain silver and gold by trading with us. They will pass us and go to the interior lands—"

"No!" Shamgar interrupts. "Their goddess has told them to destroy us. It is her will."

"Who said this? Their king?" Meshullam asks.

Nahor says, "The King of Gath is there, but he let a woman speak for him. She said she was the Handmaiden of Ashtoreth." Nahor hesitates. "She was . . . like nothing I have seen."

"It makes no sense!" someone says, and others say the same thing all around the room.

Shamgar is at the end of his patience. Wants to storm out of the room, cursing them all as cowards, wants to beat to death the next man who says it 'does not make sense.' He tries to be heard over the noise until, in frustration, he yells out, "I will face them!"

The clamor dies and they stare at him.

"You are not a champion," Zebulun says. The disdain in his voice forces Shamgar to control his temper.

"Forgive my debts to you and I will face them," Shamgar says.

"I will do no such thing."

"Your city will burn, and you with us."

Meshullam holds up his hand to Zebulun, silencing him. He hobbles up to Shamgar with his cane.

"We must evacuate," Meshullam says. "Retreat to the central hills, to Benjamin or Judah."

"If you leave the city they will pursue us and kill every man, woman, and child. Our only chance is to hold our city until others in Israel can help us," Nahor says.

"We can serve them as slaves," one of the men says. "They might allow it."

There is more yelling back and forth until Meshullam quiets them down. He looks at Shamgar.

"Have you ever fought men?"

"I live on the frontier. I have fought with bandits."

"You have seen their champion?"

"They have several. Some for Dagon and some for Ashtoreth. She said we may send a man for each of them."

Meshullam looks at Zebulun. "You have strong fighters in your guard. Send them."

"They will be protecting me."

"You cannot spare *any* of them?"

"No."

"Not even a single one?"

Zebulun shakes his head. "No." He looks around at the furious expression on the other men. "But . . . if the farmer prevails against them, I will postpone the debt."

"You will cancel the debt," Meshullam says.

Zebulun scowls at him. "Very well. If he prevails I will cancel the debt. When he dies, his wife and children become my property."

"His wife and children will labor for you, but they will not become your property," Meshullam answers. Zebulun sighs. Then nods.

Shamgar bows his head in gratitude as relief floods him. "Thank you, lord."

"I will go with Shamgar," Nahor says.

"Are there so few men left in Israel?" Meshullam asks the room, exasperated. "These men have families."

He paces for a moment, his walking staff thumping on the stone and echoing in the room. He looks at Shamgar.

"If you can delay them even a day, that will give us time to prepare the city."

Shamgar knows the time has come. He gathers himself.

"My lords, I have seen this day coming for many months. A messenger has been appearing to me and warning me, and then I believed I saw a blood moon, their sign for war. But, no one else saw it, and I was convinced I was going mad. Now they are coming, just as the messenger said."

"Who is this messenger?" Meshullam asks.

"I do not know. But he has been correct."

Nahor frowns at him. "But there *was* a blood moon. It was last month on the plains. A merchant told me. We did not see it here, but they saw it in Philistine lands."

Shamgar suddenly feels like he will collapse with relief. He understands, finally, that he saw what he needed to see, when he needed to see it, and that he has not gone mad. It *was* a vision.

"The messenger said that we would prevail if we faced them in the boundary. Your god will give victory," he says.

Zebulun laughs aloud at this, and many of the other elders do so as well. Meshullam eventually quiets them.

"Our god? The silent one? The absent one? You understand why we might be unwilling to believe you," he says.

Shamgar nods. "I understand. But it is the word of your god, and everything he has told me until now has been true. I will no longer tolerate living near dangerous roads, with my family unable to fetch water from a community well."

"Our people only know stories of our god."

"That is why he has returned to remind you, and to save you."

After a moment, Meshullam walks over to the table and leans on it to pull off his sandal. He holds the sandal up to everyone to the room.

"This council witnesses the oath of Zebulun to forgive the farmer's debts if he holds them long enough to let us build our defenses," Meshullum says.

"We witness it," came the reply from all of them, and more men hold up their own sandals.

✥ 18 ✥

As Shamgar and Nahor remain in the council room, the city outside bursts into frantic activity when word spreads of the invasion. Barricades are hastily erected across doorways and at the gate, and people scurry about, gathering food and making trips to the well. Anxious murmuring of families huddling together, the sound of hurried footsteps echoing through narrow streets. Mothers clutch their children tightly, their faces pale with fear, while men fortify their homes with whatever they can find.

When he steps outside, Shamgar is surprised to see all of this. People are sheep, his father always told him; happy to be ignorant about wolves as long as possible, then suddenly flee in terror when they are close.

Shamgar returns to the inn with Nahor. Outside the door, Nahor says, "I will say goodbye to my family and wait for you at the gate," then continues on.

Shamgar stands in front of the door, his hand hovering over it. Finally, he gets the strength to reach out and knock.

The innkeeper opens it. Her usual coy, confident expression is gone.

"We have heard. You are going alone?"

CHAPTER 18

"Nahor is coming as well. He is a good man."

She looks out at the bustling courtyard, where everyone is desperately preparing for the siege, then back to him.

"I knew, better than most, that the men of this city are weak," she says. "Your family can stay here."

Shamgar bows his head gratefully. "I cannot pay you."

"If we survive, I will make sure the cowards who did not join you provide for them." Her smile now is genuine. Perhaps even respectful.

"Thank you."

She steps aside and lets him in. He follows her down a corridor into a dining room, where his son and daughter are waiting.

"Papa!" his daughter cries as she runs to him. He picks her up.

His wife comes in, but stops when she sees him. After a long moment she says, "What will you do?"

"The elders have forced Zebulun to forgive my debt if I can hold them off long enough to let the city prepare."

Anger flashes across her face. "No one else will go with you?"

"Nahor said he would go."

"Who is Nahor?"

"A man I know in the city. A good man."

She nods. Looks at the innkeeper a moment, then back to Shamgar. "I...would rather you live than be free of the debt."

He clenches his teeth, unsure of what to say.

After a moment she walks up to him, and he pulls her in and holds her. The innkeeper remains quiet in the corner of the room.

Shamgar braces himself, looking into his daughter's face, then his son's. The boy is trying to appear stoic and brave in front of the women in the room.

"You will stay here, our host has offered you room and board," he says.

His wife steps back and says, "We are going with you."

"The only chance you have to live is to stay behind the wall in the city and—"

"You will kill their champion and we will be waiting for you at home."

She says this with such simplicity and confidence that he has no immediate answer.

"Children, grab our things," she says, and the two of them leave the room.

"You need to stay, the innkeeper has very kindly offered this to you."

His wife draws close to him again. She places her hands on his face and makes him look down at her. "You have been foolish in many things, but you were given a vision from Yahweh. I believe he gave it to you because you are the *only man* in this valley. You will kill their champion, and we will be at home expecting you to return."

{ 19 }

MESHULLAM IS WAITING for them at the gate. A group of city elders are with him, along with the watch commander. Even from a distance, Shamgar can see that both of the older men are furious.

"The council has decided that every available weapon must remain here for the defense of the city," Meshullam says, unable to hide his disgust as he looks at the others. "I know I promised you a sword, but panic has taken over."

Shamgar takes a moment. Then, holding out his oxgoad, he grins and says, "This can tear flesh as well as a blade."

"I would go with you, but I have been ordered to remain and prepare for the siege," the watch commander says bitterly. "I know we could prevail together."

Shamgar acknowledges him with a slight bow.

"Your family needs to stay here," Meshullam says, noticing them at last.

"My lord, it seems you would need to chain them."

"Be reasonable."

His wife says, "My lord, thank you for your concern, but we are leaving as a family, and my husband will save your city."

Meshullam cannot help but smile at her. He faces the group. "Here is what Israelites used to be!"

Nahor approaches from the other side of the courtyard, and next to him is Zebulun, along with a dozen men of his personal guard. Nahor's expression is dour, and Shamgar braces himself.

"You are not taking a city elder with you, farmer," Zebulun says between heavy breaths.

Shamgar turns to Nahor. "Is this true?"

Nahor shifts nervously on his feet. He glances at the other elders.

"I am afraid I cannot join you. I am needed here."

A sinking, hollow feeling settles in Shamgar's gut. He waits for Nahor to meet his eyes again. Knows he will not.

"How did Zebulun take your heart, Nahor? What did he promise?"

"It is not that simple."

"You saw them in the boundary! You know what she said they will do."

"Shamgar, I have a family, you have a family—"

Shamgar's wife walks up to Nahor and strikes him on the face. Without pausing, she turns to Zebulun and slaps him hard as well.

Zebulun stumbles backwards, his face turning red with fury.

"Stone her now!" he yells. His guards reach out to seize her.

"You will do no such thing," the watch commander says, "or you will need to stone me also, because I will cut you in half if you touch that woman."

"This is outrageous, allowing a woman to—"

Meshullam raises his walking staff to block Zebulun's guards. "No one is stoning anyone. If you speak again, Zebulun, I will have you flogged."

Zebulun does try to speak again, but the watch commander steps in front of him with his hand on his sword.

Meshullam lowers his head. Somewhere a child is crying, and

donkeys are braying as their owners hurry to stow them before the siege, and across the city other sounds of fear fill the air.

Shamgar looks around at all of them, then at Meshullam.

"When this day is written, tell them a farmer stood alone in the boundary."

He gestures at his wife.

"And tell them that a woman had more courage than every man in this city."

Meshullam clenches his teeth. Glares at the other elders.

"It will be written. I vow it."

Shamgar nods and gestures for his family to follow him through the gate.

"Shamgar son of Anath," Meshullam says behind him. Shamgar turns.

Meshullam places his hand on Shamgar's shoulder. Holds it there a long moment, and tilts his head to see him through his good eye.

"In the old days our fathers prayed for the blessing of Yahweh on a man going to face his death. I speak that blessing now, in the name of the God of Abraham, Isaac, and Jacob."

$\maltese$ 20 $\maltese$

It is late afternoon when they arrive at the beginning of the pass, where the road narrows between the cliffs. Shamgar halts them. The trail to his home is nearby. This is where he must part with his family.

Clouds have lifted above the peaks. He can see further east now, where the valley bends.

The dead girl is in front of them, and on the other side of her is the Philistine army, seemingly endless.

When his wife sees them, she lets out a small gasp of fright, then steadies herself.

The Philistines have been standing very still, as though summoned from the clay of the earth and sculpted by gods, but now they are moving, led by the Handmaiden.

"Are those the Philistines, papa?" his son asks.

"They are. You must go now," he says quietly.

His wife's hand finds his elbow and she draws close to him.

"What will you do?" she asks.

"I do not know yet," he says, then looks at his children. "Wait here while I speak with your mother."

She takes his hand willingly and follows him a short distance away.

CHAPTER 20

He positions himself with his back to the children. Tears are covering his wife's face, but she is not sobbing; instead she is clenching her teeth together and looking back and forth from the Philistines to Shamgar.

"You will defeat them," she says.

He cups his hands around her neck firmly.

"My love, you must listen to me carefully."

"*No!* You will prevail!"

He remains quiet as he looks at her. And now he understands —as she understands.

"I will prevail," he says gently.

A sob finally comes, and another, and he lets her weep. He joins her, his own tears falling hot and wet onto her hair—for a simple life together lost, and his son never growing to manhood, and his daughter never bearing children.

She gathers herself at last. He reaches into his belt and pulls out the shearing dagger with a trembling hand.

"For the children, stab here." He points the tip to her neck. "Sever deep in this place. It will be less pain, and as the blood drains they will fall asleep. It will be peaceful. But you must press hard, as hard as you can. Do you understand?"

She nods.

"For yourself, you must cut in a different place." He holds up the tip to the base of his ear and demonstrates a slashing motion. "You must cut deep enough to ensure death. Do you understand?"

She starts to say something, but stops herself. Her eyes are fixed on his. Frustrated, he grabs her arm and shakes her.

"You *cannot* survive the cut. They will show you no mercy if you survive. They will show no mercy to our daughter. Do you understand?"

"I understand," she says. She buries her face in his chest again. He smells her hair as he inhales deeply; no scent of myrrh or any other soft spices; only the scent of the frontier and hard labor.

The Philistines are closer; almost in arrow range.

"I am so terribly sorry," is all he can say.

She looks up at him. Steadies herself.

"How will I know?"

Shamgar smiles. Points at the approaching Handmaiden. "I will bring you her head."

She laughs. His favorite part of life is her laugh.

"I will wait until the very last moment," she says. "I am prepared to end our lives. But those are not my final words to you."

Now she looks at him—with pride. With honor. With a fierce love he has not seen from her in years.

She bends down and picks up an ice-covered stone from the path, then grabs his cloak with her other hand.

"This is the rock your blood will cover. Do not retreat beyond it."

SHAMGAR WATCHES her lead the children away. His son waves, and he returns it. His daughter's face is pressed against her mother. His chest has a tightening feeling, and he lets himself sob a few more times to get the rest of it out. In another moment they are around the edge of the cliff and out of sight.

He turns to face the Philistines in the pass. The oxgoad is planted in the snow in front of him, and he picks it up.

YESTERDAY MORNING all he knew was keeping his oxen warm and his hens fed, and paying a debt to a cruel man. Now . . .

Shamgar looks at the countless Philistine soldiers standing before him.

Even from here he can see their mocking smiles and hear their laughter. They know it is only him in the pass. It will be entertainment for them to get a break from the monotony of the march and watch their champions cut him down.

Here he stands against them with . . . an oxgoad. A tool to herd stubborn animals. And he thinks this is a valid weapon? The absurdity of it makes him shake his head.

The king is now in front. His armor is ornate with the images of their sea god Dagon, and his beard is woven with amulets of gold and silver. A shield bearer stands next to him holding a large scimitar and shield.

Next to the king are two women: the Handmaiden of Ashtoreth, and a younger one who appears to be an acolyte. She has fair skin and light hair, probably from the far northern islands of the Great Sea. He has seen those who resemble her as they passed on the trade road.

The two women are wearing ornamental robes. Their hair is

decorated with gold weavings. Amulets dangle from their bracelets and necklaces.

He has heard that girls are taken from their homes while children to serve as temple prostitutes in Gath. They come of age being violated dozens of times every day in the dark and smoke-filled corridors of the temples, parts of their soul torn away with every rough man who handles them.

Now, they are demons. Nightmares clothed in seductive flesh. Their eyes stay on him as they walk casually past the king, and they are leading a little girl.

She is a Hebrew, around ten years old and shabbily dressed. Probably taken from one of the villages in the lower valleys. The Handmaiden leads her along gently as they approach him.

When the group is about thirty paces from him, they stop. For a moment, nothing happens.

Then the king lifts up a hand, and a commotion behind them reveals four priests emerging from the ranks of soldiers. They are carrying a large idol on litter poles, and it is a hideous thing; the god Dagon entwined with a female figure—Ashtoreth.

They carry the idol until it is close enough for Shamgar to touch with the oxgoad. He crouches, waiting for an attack, but the priests only set the idol down reverently and step away from it.

The Handmaiden begins chanting, her voice a low, haunting melody that fills the air. She is soon joined by the acolyte, their voices intertwining in a rhythmic cadence. The priests add their deep, resonant tones, creating a layered harmony of incantations and curses in their tongue.

As the chant reaches a crescendo, the Handmaiden raises her voice sharply, a piercing note that cuts through the air. The priests follow her lead, their voices booming in unison. They all raise their hands, the gesture synchronized and deliberate. With a sudden, forceful motion, they drop their hands, the sound of their voices abruptly halting.

The sudden absence of sound is jarring. They stare at Shamgar.

Sweat gathers in his eyes. He rubs them. Forces his lips into a grin. He will not let them have the satisfaction of seeing him afraid.

The Handmaiden returns his grin with a smile of her own. She leads the Hebrew girl forward. Slowly, seductively, she pulls a long dagger out from under a slit in her robe.

The Handmaiden gingerly touches the girl's head, keeping the dagger discreetly at her side. Her fingers run through the girl's soft hair, combing it. The girl looks up at her, smiling at the tender gesture.

The acolyte drifts nearby, shadowing the Handmaiden, her movements elegant, and she appears to float over the snow.

The dagger moves quickly. The next thing Shamgar sees is an eruption of blood from the girl's throat.

The cut is so deep that the girl is unable to react. She can only look at Shamgar in confusion. His resolve fails and he looks away.

The Handmaiden grips the girl's hair tightly to hold her up until death comes. The Handmaiden watches Shamgar's reaction closely. The dead girl eventually sags in her grip.

"The virgin's blood as an offering," the acolyte says in the Philistine tongue, and the Handmaiden finally lets the girl's corpse drop against the idol.

The King of Gath raises his arms to the sky.

"May the god who dwells on this ground prevail."

The ranks of soldiers behind them burst out in cheers and calls. The king smiles broadly as he and his armor bearers walk back to them.

Only the Handmaiden remains where she is, still watching Shamgar.

～

SHAMGAR KNEELS and lays the oxgoad on the ground. More sweat trickles down his forehead. He wipes it away. The cheers of the Philistine army fade. All are waiting for him.

He looks at the oxgoad. It is not a weapon; too heavy to swing, too dull to stab through garments into flesh. It is a herding instrument for cattle. That is all.

But, it belongs to *him*. It comes from *his* farm, where he lives with *his* family, on land where *his* father and grandfather labored.

He lets the fear settle in. No fighting it. Only waiting for it to make its home. His senses are sharp. His eyes close. He breathes. He opens them and stares at the Handmaiden.

Whispers to himself: "If you are there, god of the Hebrews, this is the time to make yourself known."

He looks down at the stone his wife left him. The rock his blood will cover.

Then he stands, the oxgoad held low in his right hand.

The Handmaiden moves to him, and the acolyte follows.

Shamgar braces himself.

"Reveal your god," the king says.

"He is not a god of stone or wood. You know this," Shamgar answers.

The Handmaiden is close now. Shamgar lifts his oxgoad and points it at her. "Not another step."

The Handmaiden stops. Seems to be holding back a laugh.

"Your god sent *you* against our champion?"

"I will fight him whenever he is ready."

"You? The Hebrew champion?"

"I am the one he sent."

The Handmaiden lets herself laugh now, and the acolyte joins her, mimicking everything she is doing.

"His ways are strange," she says. She speaks softly, like she is joining him in a bedroom. "You are not a Hebrew."

"I am not."

"Why are you here? Are there no warriors in Israel?"

"This has been my family's land since my father's father."

The acolyte walks slowly to his side and leans in. She inhales deeply.

"Was that your wife and children we saw with you a moment ago?"

The Handmaiden moves close as well. The frost of her breath drifts across his face.

Shamgar leans away from them. "Send your champion."

The Handmaiden smiles. "Declare the surrender of your god and we will pass over your home."

The acolyte walks behind him and runs her hand across his back.

"Send your champion," Shamgar says again.

The acolyte presses herself against his arm as the Handmaiden drifts to his other side.

The Handmaiden says, "The Hebrews you defend will not even know your name when you die here. Come with us. Then return to your farm safely."

She places her hand on his chest and whispers, "Stand aside and you will be with us tonight. You will know pleasure you have never known."

Shamgar breathes her in. He feels dizzy. Then he looks down at the Hebrew girl's body. His feet are touching the edge of her pool of blood in the snow. He braces himself, looking for courage.

"I know your ways. You cannot proceed until you know your gods control this ground, and your champion must defeat me here to prove it. If I stand aside, you will kill my family regardless."

"Ah, but those are the old ways," she says, the smile warmer than ever. He sees her eyes more closely now, black where they should be white. "Ashtoreth can persuade. Ashtoreth can join together. She whispers to Dagon in their bedchamber, and he does her bidding. I am her most loyal servant, and she honors my obedience. Ashtoreth the abundant, the fertile, the life-giving, has allowed me to show mercy on whom I wish."

In a flicker of a moment, Shamgar considers it, because how could he not? The fear of pain, of bloody death for his family. The women together, a pleasure he would never know.

Finally, he manages to say, "Send your champion."

"Who was your father?" the Handmaiden asks.

"A simple man named Anath, who farmed the ground you see and died poor. But he held it all of his life, and he would come back from the land of the dead and flog me if I surrendered it to Philistines."

"You would die for Hebrew filth? How predictable of them, that they would run away as cowards and let a foreigner defend them."

"If the Hebrew god chooses to use me, so be it."

For the first time, the two women appear hesitant. They look past Shamgar, as though searching for something behind him.

As he waits for their response, Shamgar studies the Philistine army. Each of the men carries a sword, and there are javelins, spears, archers and slingers.

The King of Gath is losing his patience and says, "This is your last opportunity. Yield the god-challenge and keep your life."

Shamgar feels doubt returning. They might be lying . . . but they might not. How is he to know they will leave, even if he prevails?

"Send your champion," Shamgar says. He steps back and holds the oxgoad in both hands.

THE HANDMAIDEN MAKES A SMALL GESTURE. There is commotion in the ranks as the troops part, revealing a warrior wearing a helmet with thick horsehair plumes, a burnished iron breastplate, and carrying an iron scimitar. Iron is everywhere Shamgar looks in their army, but this man is covered from head to foot with it. Emerging with him is an armor bearer carrying a long javelin and a shield.

The soldiers give a series of rhythmic shouts, clanging their weapons on their shoulders as the champion raises his arm to acknowledge them; an arm covered with intricate tattoos.

To Shamgar's surprise, the champion is not a giant; he is no larger than any other soldier, but there is something elegant in his movements, in how his feet easily find their footing on rock and ice, how his arms fluidly sweep side to side. Immense control over hidden strength.

He is a prince of warriors, a god to be worshipped.

Shamgar holds the oxgoad up, its handle now slick with sweat.

Hebrew god, I am here as you commanded. Be with me.

THE CHAMPION WALKS to his left. Shamgar pivots to follow him.

Suddenly the sword flashes and knocks aside the oxgoad, and the Philistine rushes in to strike Shamgar with his other hand.

Shamgar ducks away, missing most of the force of the blow, but he loses his balance on the snow and falls. As he tries to get up the Philistine champion steps on his oxgoad handle with one foot and kicks Shamgar in the head with the other.

Shamgar feels the world spin and his ears ring. He tries to roll over but the champion's weight is pinning him down.

To the sound of cheering, the Philistine kneels on Shamgar's chest. He leans in close.

"What is the sign of submission for your people?"

Shamgar wrenches against him but cannot get away, instead sinking deeper into the snow.

The Philistine presses the tip of his sword into Shamgar's ear. He twists it slowly.

Shamgar grimaces. Feels blood streaming down his neck.

"Show me the sign of submission for your people."

Terror emerges again, gnaws at him, chokes him. There is no one else here. No power. No strength. No salvation.

Shamgar nods slightly. The Philistine eases the pressure on him, and Shamgar slides his left hand out. He places it on the back of the Philistine's thigh and holds his right hand out open-palm.

"The Hebrew is giving their sign of submission," the Philistine says loudly.

Another strong round of cheers from the soldiers. Shamgar recoils as the champion leans close again.

"I heard legends of the Hebrew god. I see they were false."

He pats Shamgar on the side of his head.

"You were brave to face me. Tell me where your home is and I will ensure it is spared. Your wife will be my concubine and your children will be my slaves."

Shamgar blinks away a tear forming in his eye. All is a lie. All is empty.

✺ 23 ✺

THE CHAMPION STANDS UP, releasing the pressure on the farmer. He turns to his army.

"The Hebrew is now my slave," he shouts, holding up the oxgoad, and they cheer for him. He tosses the oxgoad aside. Looking at the Handmaiden, he says, "He and his family belong to me. See to it they are spared."

"Blasphemous," the Handmaiden answers. "You must kill him."

"They are my spoils."

"Ashtoreth does not want any to survive."

The champion takes off his helmet and holds it in front of her. "This is the signet of Dagon. It means I serve him, not your Ashtoreth. He grants me this spoil, and your goddess will submit."

The Handmaiden feels her rage growing, but catches herself. Patience. As with all things, patience.

She bows her head to acknowledge him. "You are worthy of great spoils. There are many more to gain. Now we must—"

She is interrupted by a noise and turns to face it.

The farmer is crawling away, oxgoad in hand, and as soon as he is on his feet he starts to run.

"Stop him!" the Handmaiden yells.

"I have done my part of this, witch," the champion says, then walks back into the ranks.

The acolyte starts to follow the champion, but the Handmaiden stops her by shaking her head, imperceptible to anyone else.

"This means we proceed?" the King of Gath asks.

The Handmaiden watches the farmer running away. She inhales a long breath, her eyes closed.

A shadow passing. The wind above reaches the trees, and snow swirls from the boughs. She listens very carefully . . .

She opens her eyes again.

"We must kill him first."

"He yielded to our champion."

She turns on him. "The Hebrew god is full of trickery and deceit. Ashtoreth demands the farmer as a sacrifice."

The king sighs. He gestures for one of his commanders to approach. The commander kneels at his feet with his head bowed.

"Capture him."

❦ 24 ❦

SHAMGAR RUNS, snow kicking up, ice in his face, the wind making him stagger. He puts his hand down to steady himself, dragging the oxgoad behind him. He kneels down. Holds his breath. Listens.

Shouts behind and above. He crouches against a bush. Listens again.

Someone is yelling orders above him. He hears boots tramping down the slope nearby.

He holds the oxgoad and waits.

A Philistine appears from around the bush. Shamgar swings the heavy tool as hard as he can, striking the man's chest and knocking him over.

Shamgar rushes away from the bush, hearing the grunts of the Philistine's companions as they pursue him. He scrambles across another small rise, leaps down the other side and slides into a steep embankment. At the bottom is a tiny stream. The shock of the cold water makes him gasp. It revives him enough to get back to his feet and keep running.

He hears men splash into the water behind him. Down the shallow stream, then a hard turn as he climbs up the slope again.

Shamgar falls many times as he runs, his knees scraped raw from the ice, his ear bleeding. Still he runs, knowing he should feel humiliation but no longer caring.

And then the very air around him tears open.

A hissing of arrow blades passing his ears, the yelling of men, he is tripping backwards and falling into the snow.

He rolls to his side. Arrows thud into the ground where he was laying a moment before.

An arrow slices through the flesh of his leg, and though he does not feel the burning pain he expects, he panics that it has severed something deep.

The arrows stop. There is confusion. Someone is trying to give orders, but there are too many men shouting and orders cannot be heard. Shamgar lurches to his left and finds his feet. Somehow the oxgoad is still in his hand.

A javelin shakes him out of his stupor when it hits his leg. These are used by infantry when an enemy closer than arrow range. He winces and pulls it out. He throws it wildly in the general direction of the Philistines, and then he is up and running at last, his legs finally obeying his mind's pleas, and through the snow and ice on the path his boots find footing.

The forest on the other end of the pass is close. His knees stiffen from the swelling of the wounds, making him stumble. He stays upright by planting the oxgoad with each step. Another arrow hits near his foot.

Pure terror in his heart, the kind he knew as a boy when the dark night bled through the window of his home and brought the sound of the jackals. It did not matter that his father was in the next room, he only knew they were *there,* and their jaws would clamp around his throat before he could scream for help.

The trees swallow him. He cries out in relief to finally have something between him and the enemy. The oxgoad gets snagged in some bramble. He yanks on it. The hook is caught. He yanks harder.

Shouts from the Philistines. An officer giving orders. He holds still. Thinks about laying down and trying to hide in the snow.

Madness. They saw him run into the woods, they know precisely where he is.

He pulls desperately at the oxgoad until it finally rips out of the root.

He is moving again. Slower now. The undergrowth is snagging his feet.

An arrow strikes his shoulder so hard that his breath catches. He glances, expecting to see the tip buried all the way in, but there is nothing there. He stops a moment. Confusion. Why did the arrow not . . .

Then there is a sudden rush of wind. Bits of ice pelt his face. A snowstorm rushes in fast, much faster than it should, and this, too, confuses him. Impossible. What is happening? Whatever it is, it has caused bewilderment among the Philistines as well. He can no longer see them through the wind-blown flakes, which means they could not see him, either.

"Keep moving, keep moving, keep moving."

Talking to himself makes him keep running, makes him stay just out of reach of the Philistines.

But the air is torn open again as arrows pour through the trees. They are releasing them blindly. No javelins, though, and he feels a surge of hope that he has gained distance.

A stone hits him in the scalp. A burst of light. Then darkness. Blindness. A stone?

He feels warm liquid stream into his eyes. He rubs at them with his fingers. He finally sees light through a haze of red. The blood makes its way to his mouth. He spits it out. It takes him a moment to piece together what is happening.

They are slinging stones at him. Stones and arrows are everywhere, his entire world, all he knows. The sky opens up with as many stones as snowflakes. All he can do is curl up like an infant and hold his knees to his chest and cover his face with his hands. They are striking his flesh repeatedly and he feels his knuckles getting crushed.

The rocks stop falling.

Why are they waiting? Refilling their slings? They cannot actually see him. The Philistines must be sending volleys into the forest where they saw him flee.

He is light-headed. Feels something vaguely painful and touches his forehead.

Part of his scalp hangs in a flap over one eye. It is swelling so fast that his eye is closing.

He pulls up the oxgoad tip. Using the small bladed edge of the hook, he slices the flesh above his eyelid to drain blood. That is not enough, the swelling is too heavy.

He calms himself with steady breathing. Then, starting with the corner of the flesh on his scalp, he starts cutting away the entire flap of skin hanging over his eye. Hot, searing pain makes his hand shake as he works, but he presses on until a portion of flesh the size of his palm is sliced away. The raw wound, exposed to air, burns so badly that tears well in his eyes, but now he can see. He just needs to be able to see.

Using the oxgoad to pull himself up, Shamgar squints through the blood, trying to see where the soldiers are.

Nothing but thick snowfall. He can hear them talking. A few shouted commands.

Shamgar turns to flee. Behind him, then over him, then all around him come the rocks. He covers his scalp with his free hand. The snow is too deep to run through, so he must leap and trudge. Rocks pummel all around him.

He feels the volley slow down, believes it has passed, but then there is a sudden crushing strike on his back as a rock finds him. It knocks his air out and he falls into a snow bank.

All he can muster is a gagging groan. He fumbles for the oxgoad. His fingers find the staff and he pulls it close. Hugs it like a child hugs a toy.

"Get up. Get up now," he mutters through bleeding lips.

On his feet. He shakes away the snow and staggers forward again.

He comes to a slope and pauses to study the terrain ahead.

The brush clears up considerably, but so does his concealment. He will be able to move faster. He will also be exposed.

There is no choice, then. If he can get higher up, perhaps they will continue pursuing him, and if they are pursuing *him*, they are not approaching his home.

Step by painful step he climbs the hill. Rocks and arrows occasionally land near him, but his energy to climb is increased by his terror.

And then rage boils up, shocking him, and he screams, "Where were you? I obeyed! I believed you and you left me to die!" He continues shouting this to the indifferent clouds above.

At the top of the hill he emerges into a meadow. He trudges to the edge of a stone ledge overlooking the pass and collapses to his knees.

Suddenly, as though it has been waiting for him to reach this spot, the storm clears. Shielding his eyes, he tries to make out the Philistine movements in the pass.

In the middle is the Handmaiden and the idol. Her acolyte nearby. They have their arms raised, still calling down curses on him.

The priests are next to the king. The rest of the army stretches far through the pass, seemingly endless numbers of them.

And yet . . . they are not marching. Not until their gods have seen him die as a sacrifice. When he does, no gods will resist them in the land as they rampage at will.

He has always loved this ledge. From here he can spot a missing sheep in the north fields, or check for predators lurking in the pass. When the sea breeze arrives up here in the late afternoons of summer, it is the most peaceful place in his land.

Unable to avoid it longer, Shamgar finally lets himself look far to his left, across the treetops to the end of the pass where he can see the rooftop of his house. A pale wisp of smoke seems to appear, but he cannot determine if it is a trick of his eyes.

Keep the fire stoked and the coal beds hot, he had told her on the way to the boundary, so that when they come you can quickly set the home on fire. The dagger blade was as sharp as he could make it on the sharpening stone. It would slice cleanly.

He looks away from the house. Sweat burns in the scalp wound. Each strike from the rocks, arrows, and darts is making itself known, as though his wounded body is demanding to be accounted for in his thoughts.

He searches the hillside below for pursuing troop movements. Nothing at first . . . then a movement. Then another. Then another. More.

His breath catches.

So many more.

Like ants emerging from their lair.

He watches the Philistine troops as they move between the trees, carefully making their way up the hill to his position, and he knows there is nothing that can be done about it.

They will reach him, and he will die.

The thought comes to return to his home. To run back as fast as his legs will carry him and grab his wife and children and retreat further into the hill country, perhaps find a caravan that will take them to Assyria, even Damascus itself, where he can live his life in peace and herd cattle.

He lets his head fall in weariness. His reason returns. He can do no such thing. They will be run down like everyone else. No way to move two young children fast enough to escape hardened soldiers looking for rape and blood.

No, he will stay here and die in the pass, and his wife and children will die as well. At least Zebulun will have his fat belly slit by a Philistine, and Shamgar delights in this thought.

He laughs at himself through his parched throat. One man against an army. What a fool he was.

But . . . there was no choice. There remains no choice. Perhaps the Hebrew god could have appeared. That had been their only hope.

The Philistines are moving faster up the hill now, emboldened by his bloody trail. Soon they will be at the summit.

It is all very clear what will happen. He will make his stand on this rock and they will cut him down, and as his blood flows into the earth, their gods will be satiated, and they will know they can cross the Boundary of Blood with no interference from any Hebrew god. Dagon and Ashtoreth will rule this land.

He feels a thump as something hits his back, but there is no pain, and it confuses him. Then he feels another thump, still no pain, and then a third one, and that brings a torrent of agony as it penetrates his cloak. He realizes that arrows are hitting the snow all around him. As he runs he feels his right shoulder stiffening. He cannot move his arm--realizes his shoulder blade is blocked from moving because an arrow is lodged next to his spine. He reaches back for it, trying to rip it out. Cannot reach it.

In desperation he rubs his back against a tree, trying to dislodge it. This only forces it in further, and something pinches deep in his lungs, hot like fire, and he cries out in fear. He has pressed the arrow in too far—*he will die.*

The voices emerge again, and Shamgar turns abruptly towards the steepest slope he can find. He tries to climb up but the snow is deep here. He cannot push through it.

He turns to his left, sees a small break in the brush where a game trail exists, and staggers along it.

An arrow hits the snow near his feet. He hears another twang from another bow, and that arrow strikes his arm. They are right behind him.

He pulls the arrow out from his arm; it is a shallow wound and it comes out easily, does not hurt. Nothing hurts like the arrow in his back, and he coughs, sees blood, panics, decides again that he is a dead man.

Get higher. Get higher.

Somehow, he gets further up the slope. His legs are failing. Glances back, sees the Philistines pursuing, closing in.

Finally he is on the top of a ridge, the valley spread out below him. He can see the snaking formation of Philistine soldiers in their dark winter cloaks and iron helmets. Sees the Handmaiden and her acolyte and the king near their idol, looking up at him. They spot him highlighted against the sky.

He no longer cares.

Along this ridge he will reach his home. He will continue bleeding, slowly dying, but he feels he will make it to his home. Burst into the room. End the life of his children himself, to prevent his wife from needing to do so. Then he will end her life, quickly and with only brief pain. He will hold her, apologize one final time, ask forgiveness one final time.

Then he will turn the blade on himself, and all will be black. All will be at peace.

The wind howls. Ice in his face, his breath sharp and biting.

Through a gap in the trees he sees it; his home in the small clearing. His barn. His land. Only a day ago, they were his.

Shouts behind him. He turns. The Philistines are closing in quickly. They have reached the top of the ridge and see him.

Shamgar tries to keep running but his legs feel numb. His head faint.

Blood loss, but he cannot let it stop him, he must keep moving.

And then he knows, *feels*, there is not enough blood left in him to make it. Too far away. His wife and children too far away.

Press the blade firm and deep, my love. It will be fast. Do not miss the veins.

He slowly stops running, then walking. He goes to his knees. The sharpness of the ache in his back dulls. His ears ring and his head feels too light to hold up any longer.

Shamgar lets the oxgoad drop to his side. He wonders if they will kill him here, quickly, or drag him back to their idols.

As he waits, he looks one more time at the small home in the woods. The hard days. Many, many hard days. An unforgiving land. But there were good days, too.

He hears the snap of a sling releasing a stone, hears the whistle as the stone flies towards him, the strike against his head, and then there is nothing but darkness.

PART IV

$$\approx \quad 2\,5 \quad \approx$$

THE DARKNESS LASTS A MOMENT. Quiet. Still. He feels nothing anymore, no pain. He is beyond the land now, the place of the dead. Sheol, they called it.

And is this it? For eternity? To drift in darkness?

But then a flickering noise on his left comes and he feels himself able to turn and look at it. He still has his body. He sees a flame, a small one, the size of an oil lamp. His eyes adjust and he sees that it is actually a large fire, but far away.

He wonders if he can go to it. Feels something like earth underneath him and he takes a step. As he moves he notices more of his body. He is not a spirit at all. Now he feels cold again. And wet. He shivers.

The taste of blood in his mouth. And pain again, which upsets him. He is not dead, then?

But where is he?

He feels something warm pouring into his eye and wipes at it. Blood. He touches his scalp and finds an enormous gash. Remembers he was struck by a slinger's stone just before it became dark.

Even though he senses pain, in his lungs and on his head, he is not impeded anymore. His feet move one in front of the other and he is drawn to the firelight.

Around him it finally brightens enough to see that he is still on the ridge. Ahead is his farm.

There is a fire nearby, and a man sits next to it.

Shamgar turns around, vaguely searching for Philistines, but the forest is quiet.

He looks back at the man. It is the stranger, huddled under a winter cloak.

Shamgar makes his way to the other side of the fire and kneels. Only . . . it is not a fire like a campfire or watchfire; it is a stone altar, with flames on top of it. He cannot tell what it is burning. No smell of wood smoke; no smell of meat cooking.

The stranger watches him. Shamgar, weary of games, watches him back. If confusion is to be his lot, he is resigned to it.

"Yahweh is pleased with you," the stranger says.

Shamgar scowls at this. Yet he is no longer angry. Only confused. This, too, puzzles him. It is odd the Philistines have stopped pursuing him. His wounds bleed, pain exists, but there is no other feeling of threat. Somehow it is the stranger's presence alone that he feels.

"What will happen?"

It is the only thing Shamgar can think to ask. The stranger gives the slightest of smiles. He stands up, and as he does, the forest starts to fade away.

Rippling ice and wind all around, and the altar remains, its flames burning, but everything else slips away as though blown by a gale.

Shamgar feels the cold. Shrugs against it under his cloak. He keeps his eyes fixed on the altar and the flames upon it. Something tells him to. He does not know what.

Then he feels a ripping, a tearing, a slashing across his chest as he is devoured by something that roars.

$\maltese$ 26 $\maltese$

Then . . . all is calm.

Faint rippling sounds, like water lapping on a creek bank.

He looks down and grasps that he is standing in water up to his ankles.

A vast sea stretches away from him in every direction. On the far horizon, under a twilight sky, vast mountains stand watch in every direction, terrible and powerful.

This is the dream again, but now, he senses it is real.

A small spark of light—there and then gone.

Fully alert, he searches the darkness where the spark had been.

Another scraping noise, a flare of sparks, and Shamgar realizes he is looking at a fire being lit.

The flames grow slowly. All of time is slowing. He feels even his very heartbeat going still.

Then the fire roars to life, swirling and twisting in unnatural ways, creating something like the mirage across hazy stones on a hot day.

He changes his focus from the fire to what can be seen in its light.

There is a man standing on the edge of it, and he is looking at Shamgar.

Shamgar tries to say something but he is not certain he still has a throat to speak with.

Terror. That is what he feels. The endless depths of terror. Terror of the ages past and the ages to come, for this man has no age to him; he could be in his twentieth year or his ten-thousandth.

His beard frames a hard, scar-covered face. The marks of war wounds. Torn flesh on his scalp.

As the firelight grows, it reveals more of him—armor, and a weapon belt of some kind, but Shamgar cannot make out the forging. Shamgar's wife, his farm, everything is shrouded in distant memory. There is only this warrior next to his fire.

He is everything. He is all.

The man approaches Shamgar through the flames—flames that are coming from the top of what he now sees is a stone altar, and with the man comes a flood of dread and . . . *power*.

Something rages in the air as the stranger walks, heavy like the purple and gray storms that swallow the pass in the summer heat.

The warrior slides a blade out of his belt and in a fluid motion presses the tip into Shamgar's chest. The prickle of pain it creates is the first physical sensation Shamgar has had since he entered this . . . dream?

Shamgar is helpless to resist the blade. The man will shove it forward in a powerful stab and Shamgar's flesh will part before it like the fat of a new lamb, and all will be over, and it will be such relief that Shamgar finds himself yearning for the stranger to just finish him now.

But the warrior does not kill him yet.

He stares *into* Shamgar, the sword tip pressed painfully into his chest, and stands perfectly still.

Thoughts are in Shamgar's mind. Disconnected, but

somehow intentional. The stranger wants him to see something. He concentrates.

There is lightning on a dark sky. A river of blood across a golden desert. Fire racing to the heavens and swallowing the mountains. A chariot, its rider in gleaming armor, collapsing into a foamy raging sea. Serpents and corpses and ever more fire, until the fire consumes all around and he begins to feel it burn in his mind and into his flesh, tearing up all that he is, consuming everything but his eyes, because through his eyes he still sees the warrior watching him and feels the blade pressing harder against his chest until it finally bursts through the surface.

The blade goes all the way into his heart.

The fire from the altar comes alive and roars until it reaches the hilt of the sword, then enters the sword itself and sears through the blade into his chest.

Through the pain, Shamgar hears an ancient voice, more powerful and terrible than all:

I AM YAHWEH, THE GOD OF ABRAHAM, ISAAC, AND JACOB, AND YOU WILL CUT DOWN MY ENEMIES UNTIL EVEN THE STONES CRY OUT PRAISE TO MY NAME.

SHAMGAR IS on his ledge above the pass, just as before, but now he feels very . . . different.

Panting, sweating, pressure in his head and chest as though he is going to rip apart just by breathing.

He is suddenly compelled to jump to his feet, and he does, his movement so fierce and powerful that he nearly leaps off the ledge.

His ears discern every sound, his eyes catch every movement. Hawks high above waiting for the winter storm to pass. The whispered mutterings of Philistine soldiers and officers close by. All of these are as clear as though they are happening inside of his head. Every flash of a snowflake in the breeze and every icy stone on the mountainside is overwhelming in its clarity.

He lets out a groan like steam escaping a baking pot. His chest and arms start to twitch and jerk as his muscles seem to flood with fire itself. Yes, fire, that is what he is feeling, though he cannot see it, he only sees the pass that leads to his home and all that he loves in this life—and then the slightest sound that he should have never heard is loud and raging in his ear: the sound of an arrow being fixed into a notch.

Shamgar plunges his hand into the snow and picks up the

nearest fist-sized rock. He hurls it with all of his hate in a perfect throw towards the sound.

The stone crushes the face of the Philistine soldier who has appeared on Shamgar's ledge. He flops backwards into his partner, who finds himself covered in a spray of blood.

Shamgar looks around for a weapon—and spots the oxgoad in the snow.

He picks it up, squeezes it tight in his fingers, and runs towards the other Philistine soldier, who struggles to shove his dead friend aside and pull out his blade, but Shamgar has already reached him and buried the tip of the goad so hard into his chest that it bursts out the other side. Shamgar never slows. He rips out the hooked tip of the goad, breaking the man's ribs completely apart.

His ears hear everything. His eyes find more enemies.

At least a hundred Philistines have been sent into the forest after him and are climbing the hill. He sees them all, knows where to strike them, it all becomes perfectly clear and perfectly still for the shortest moment, until the fire rages up through his feet and legs and chest and he cannot stop himself from running down the hill into the forest.

He cuts from tree to tree, boulder to boulder. He knows every ravine and stone in this land and hides himself before striking, finding a man and then killing him, sometimes with his oxgoad, sometimes with his fists, his fingers, ramming his thumbs into eyes and breaking skulls with the oxgoad.

Shamgar moves as a spirit through the forest, careful to use the trees and boulders to his advantage, hiding when necessary and emerging to slit a throat or break a neck.

As he rushes down the hill he sees glimpses of the vast ranks of soldiers still in the pass. So many of them between him and what he loves.

You will save my people.

The voice again.

And yet it is not merely a voice. It is . . . a fire.

But he *knows* it now, knows the fire of the Ancient One, the builder of worlds, the destroyer of kingdoms, the one who has commanded him to spill every drop of Philistine blood until even the stones cry out praise to his Name.

Shamgar sees more soldiers moving through the undergrowth nearby. He cuts their legs out from under them with the oxgoad's hook.

Their screams merge with the screams of other dying men scattered throughout the woods, sounding like animals caught in snares. Like demons fleeing.

THE PHILISTINES who chased him into the trees believe that is exactly what the sound is.

They are running away from him, shouting to each other that a god-demon is in the woods.

Shamgar pursues them until he emerges out of the forest into the boundary, where the army and the Handmaiden wait for him.

❈ 28 ❈

HE SENSES SOMETHING . . . unsure what it is . . . then sees the Handmaiden standing over the corpse of the Hebrew girl.

The Handmaiden has her bare legs wrapped around the idol. He hears every curse she mutters, sees her eyes twitching back and forth under their lids. The acolyte circles her, pointing at Shamgar and speaking her own curses.

The power coils and pulses in his muscles. He finally understands what he is feeling in his spirit.

He is not merely angry. He is *offended*.

Offended that they would dare to bring false gods across the boundary of Yahweh's lands.

Behind the Handmaiden he sees the ranks of soldiers yelling and pounding their weapons on their shields, demanding the chance to fight him.

He laughs at them. Wants nothing more in this life than to stand over their corpses and taunt their gods.

"Send your champion," he says.

The King of Gath appears to be surprised that Shamgar is standing before him. Finally he raises his arm.

Three warriors emerge from the ranks. Three chosen fighters from Gath who have been drilled in warfare since childhood.

They wield three different weapons: the axe, the sword, the spear. Three souls immersed in the pagan waters of the temple and dedicated to Dagon, possessed with his wickedness. They wear nothing but loin cloths, even in winter, their chests heavily tattooed with nightmarish images of human sacrifices.

Shamgar whirls the oxgoad in his arms to feel its balance again. His blood roars hot and the scorching pain behind his eyes and across his chest rages, denying him any thought except giving the stones below the blood offering Yahweh has demanded.

The first warrior, the axe, swings his weapon savagely but darts aside when Shamgar counterattacks, ensuring that the warrior with the spear is able to make a thrust. Shamgar leaps away from it only to land directly in front of the warrior with the sword, who slashes at Shamgar's waist, making a shallow cut.

Shamgar eases back as they circle him. They coordinate their attacks, not coming at him one by one but with a unison of movements that would wear down any other fighter. Overwhelming force but also light on their feet, bobbing and weaving away from his strikes and waiting patiently for openings.

They are vastly more skilled at fighting than Shamgar, but as the moments pass and no one is able to gain ground on him, Shamgar sees where his advantage will come.

He is simply . . . not . . . tiring.

His energy is increasing, and, while they are formidable fighters, as the combat drags on, their movements are getting slower. With every swing of the oxgoad he feels a surge of strength. He is getting more powerful as the fire consumes him.

The warrior with the axe falls first. He makes an advance on Shamgar's left flank to cut low against his leg. Shamgar twists away. He manages to get enough leverage on the oxgoad to swipe the hook towards the axe warrior. The hook catches the warrior's knee and Shamgar feels it puncture deep. He plants his foot and jerks the goad back as hard as he can. The force rips away the warrior's kneecap and sinews.

CHAPTER 28

The Philistine lets out his first shout of the fight. He falls to his side, screaming for his gods. The other two have not waited to see what happens and are attacking Shamgar simultaneously. He blocks high against the sword while leaping over a stab from the spear. He blocks two more strikes. They are slower. Much slower.

He darts backwards and does a twisting leap to gain distance. The two champions are too exhausted to chase him.

Shamgar glances at the Handmaiden again. She is chanting her prayers.

He raises the oxgoad over his head and attacks the other two warriors.

They rise to meet him but their attacks are slow and he easily dodges them, rolling hard to his right and swinging the iron tip against the exposed underarm. The hook finds a notch in the man's ribs. The Philistine starts to pull away, realizes what has happened, and as his face fills with terror, Shamgar wrenches the hook with all of his might. The ribs tear away from the warrior's side.

Shamgar never stops moving and hooks the goad into the jaw of the remaining warrior. The Philistine drops his weapon.

Shamgar does not rip it out yet. He pushes the Philistine to the ground, keeping the oxgoad hooked in his jaw. Something has been severed in the man's throat and his blood is spraying freely, covering everything around them, including Shamgar.

The acolyte glares at Shamgar with deepest hatred. The Handmaiden has her eyes closed. The other two warriors are groaning at his feet nearby. The stunned army begins clamoring for his head.

Shamgar looks down at the impaled man. He leans close, careful to look him directly in his eyes, and then finally jerks the oxgoad backwards to kill him.

Rising swiftly, Shamgar walks over to the axe warrior, whose knee he destroyed, and grabs the man's hair. He pulls his head up, wanting to ensure that the man and his demon god *feel* defeat, then breaks his neck against the oxgoad handle.

The warrior with the torn ribs tries to stand up and flee, but Shamgar steps on his back.

"Renounce your god."

"Dagon will bring me in, and I will—"

The oxgoad falls so fast that the Philistine never sees it coming. The last noise he makes is a wet cough.

Shamgar steps over the corpse and positions himself in front of the idol again. He stares at the Handmaiden, then at the King of Gath.

"Send your champion again."

THE CHAMPION EMERGES AGAIN from the ranks, joined by his shield bearer. Other soldiers back away from him with their heads bowed. The most dangerous of them all, the ruler of their champions. A prince of warriors, a god to be worshipped, yes, but now Shamgar sees something else.

A man—with flesh that can be torn apart.

"I will need to kill you this time, farmer. You defied my generous offer."

The champion says this casually, in between bites of a roasted leg of lamb that he carries.

The Handmaiden begins chanting her curses, joined by the acolyte.

Shamgar listens carefully for the voice. His skin feels flush. His heart pounds. Every movement aches. The wound on his head is burning again; he feels a small trickle of blood running down his face, as though it has opened anew.

Do not abandon me.

Then, in his spirit:

It has been declared.

Pain will not ebb, and fatigue will come, but Shamgar knows —*knows*—that he has what he needs to kill this man.

Forgive me, Hebrew God, and be not offended by my doubt.

Shamgar points his oxgoad at the champion, and then at the gathered host, and says in his loudest voice, "This very day I will mount your heads on the gates of Azekah, and all the land will know there is a God in Israel."

At this, the Handmaiden stops her chanting. She turns to the champion and says something Shamgar cannot hear. The champion waves her away and approaches Shamgar with his shield bearer at his side.

And then the champion charges forward so fast that Shamgar barely has time to lift the oxgoad and block the attack, the scimitar sliding down the handle and into the hook, and Shamgar wrenches it down and away with all his might. He trips. Lands hard on his knees. Sees the scimitar arcing toward his scalp, tries to lay down beneath the blow, feels it rush past his face.

The shield bearer is attacking now, terrible and fast like his champion, and Shamgar finds himself crawling backwards through the snow to get away from their strikes.

He still has the oxgoad clenched tightly in his left hand grip. His knuckles scrape against the ice and rocks, ripping flesh. With his right he swings his fist.

Both Philistines are desperately fast and Shamgar misses, but he sees now their faces devoid of humor, their pride dissipating, and the exertion of sweat on their faces, and he knows again that they are merely men who can be torn apart.

And tear them apart he will, with a farming tool drenched in the hot blood and bile of wicked men, and his yell becomes a scream of endless fury as he strikes the heavy staff against the waist of the shield bearer. The sound of the shattering hip bone cracks across the battlefield.

The shield bearer slumps over, immobile, the shock of the blow stunning him. The champion is distracted only a breath, but this is enough, because Shamgar can move endlessly faster than any pagan champion, for he has seen the ancient fire.

The oxgoad whirls over his head, then down, striking the

champion's helmet so hard that it flies off, and then another hard blow to his face makes the man slump to his knees. Shamgar crushes his throat with the wooden handle, knocking him on his back.

Both Philistines now lay in the snow beneath him.

Shamgar wastes no further time with the shield bearer, ramming the iron tip into his neck to kill him.

As for the champion, he seizes the stunned man's boot and drags him towards the idol, glaring first at the king, then the acolyte, then the Handmaiden.

The champion tries to attack again with an aimless, feeble strike, which Shamgar easily blocks. He jabs the spike end of the handle under the man's breastplate and into his belly. This makes the Philistine lurch weakly.

Shamgar pulls him up and props him against the idol, in full view of the gathered host. He pulls away his helmet.

Blood pours out of the corners of the champion's mouth. His eyes are vague and unfocused as he looks up at Shamgar.

"Show me the sign of submission," Shamgar says.

The champion blinks. Tries to move again. Shamgar inserts the iron hook of the oxgoad into his ear.

"*Show me the sign of submission!*" he yells.

Slowly, the Philistine raises his hand and places it on Shamgar's inner thigh. With his other hand, he opens his palm.

$\maltese$ 30 $\maltese$

SHAMGAR PICKS up the champion's scimitar blade and cuts his head cleanly off with a single strike.

Quiet, now, in the Boundary of Blood.

No man speaks or moves. Not the king, not the Handmaiden —no one dares.

Shamgar drops the sword and kicks the oxgoad up from the ground into his hands. He never slows as he walks towards the two women.

The Handmaiden rises from the idol, speaking to him with deepest hatred.

"By Ashtoreth goddess of the earth, by Dagon god of the seas, you will suffer more than any man has ever suffered! Your seed will die in pain! Your woman will be ravaged by every soldier in Gath! Your land will burn and I will curse the generations beyond you!"

Shamgar stops just as he reaches her. He leans in close to her face. He wants her to see his eyes, to see what he is *feeling* . . .

. . . and . . . she does.

Feels it in the depths, senses the heat of it, the light, the ancient strength far beyond what her mind has conceived even in the black depths of the temple in Gath, when the goddess came to her as a girl.

And as she sees it, as she *feels* it, her eyes falter in terror and fear.

The oxgoad flashes up and bursts through her chest. With another strike he removes her head.

The acolyte screams at the sight of her dead mistress. She attacks, clawing at his face with her long nails.

Shamgar throws her to the ground, swinging the oxgoad and striking her in the neck. She starts gagging. He kneels down to look at her, to let her *feel* the terrible rage of the Hebrew God just as her mistress felt it.

When her body grows limp, he removes her head as well.

He holds the two heads of the women up for the King of Gath and his whole army to see.

The King of Gath keeps his bearing only a moment longer. Then he turns and flees in terror, his army fleeing with him.

Away from the pass, away from the Boundary of Blood, away from Hebrew lands, and away from the horrors they have seen.

SHAMGAR TOSSES THE HEADS ASIDE.

The fire within him calms for only a moment, long enough for him to gently carry the bodies of the Hebrew girls away from the idols of Dagon and Ashtoreth. He lays them down carefully.

He will find their families and tend to their burials. He will see the tears of their mothers and the agony of their fathers. They will tear their garments and scatter ash on their heads, and they will weep together at the evil in their land.

But first . . .

He walks back to the idol. The goddess leers at him. The blood of the sacrificed girl has stained it dark, and is flowing into the snow at its base.

Shamgar holds the oxgoad like an axe. Prays for strength,

strength to destroy whatever needs to be destroyed, and swings the oxgoad down.

The idol shatters into pieces.

He spits on its crumbled remains.

Then he raises the oxgoad up to the heavens, to the sun and the stars beyond. He yells his war cry.

Desperate to cover the rocks with more Philistine blood, he rushes after the army, feeling the might and glory of the God who rules over the Boundary of Blood.

EPILOGUE

MY KING, *now you know of the victory of Shamgar son of Anath, who is mentioned in the Song of Deborah.*

Yahweh shaped him into a mighty leader who saved our people in a desperate hour. How curious it is that he was a foreigner! When the men of God do not answer his call to war, he will find a willing heart in unlikely places.

You may recognize that mysterious fire which came over him on the battlefield. I am certain your father spoke of it, for it is how he waged war and triumphed. He knew it as the Covering.

We can imagine the glorious fright in the hearts of the Philistine kings as they heard of the awakening of Yahweh in the land.

We can envision the heads of six-hundred dead men mounted on the city walls of Azekah as a warning to the pagans, and a source of shame to weak-hearted Israelite men.

We can rejoice in the triumph over Ashtoreth, the humiliation of her priests, and the destruction of her plans to contaminate Yahweh's land with her temple.

And we can see, through the eyes of the heart, the happy reunion of Shamgar and his family, with a wife who loves him and children who admire him.

It was not long afterwards that the people of Israel once more whored against our God, and the dark years continued, but for a brief time, men found the courage of their ancestors and remembered who they were.

MAY YOUR REIGN BE LONG, *lord, and may the work of your hand prosper.*

May you remember the faith of your father David, and the faith of men like Shamgar son of Anath.

Do not turn aside to the right or to the left. Humble yourself before our mighty God, and it will go well for you.

I beg your indulgence for a word of caution: do not be seduced by the promise of safety, the strength of your chariots, or the whispers of foreign women. For as Yahweh grants you an empire, so he can remove it.

Kings of the earth are dust in his palm, and he will ensure that even the blood-covered stones cry out praise to his Name.

AFTERWORD

"After Ehud came Shamgar son of Anath, who struck down six
hundred Philistines with an oxgoad.
He too saved Israel."

JUDGES 3:31

AUTHOR'S NOTE

There is nothing known about the Biblical character of Shamgar apart from two brief references in the book of Judges, chapters 3 and 5. In this story, all characterizations and events not found in those passages are fictional, and are intended to be treated as such.

Based on careful research and time spent in the land, the details about weather, terrain, and the historical and cultural setting are generally accurate. Nonetheless, fictional choices were made to enhance the narrative and help contemporary readers relate to the journey of a man from thousands of years ago.

The Boundary of Blood is an actual pass in the foothills of Israel. Standing at the top of it, you can see where David fought Goliath, along with countless other battles in the long history of war in the region.

ACKNOWLEDGMENTS

To everyone who has dealt with me over the years: thank you for your endless grace. It has been undeserved.

To the Kavod Family Ministries team for believing in my work and being willing to take me on, warts and all.

To my wife, for confronting, challenging, persisting, and enduring.

Soli Deo gloria.